In Case We Die

In Case We Die

Edited by Aaron Dietz
and Bud Smith

Paula Bomer's "Interstitial Cystitis" first appeared in *Volume 1 Brooklyn*. Martha Grover's "The Truth about Pheromones" previously published in *Somnambulist*. Ben Loory's "I Ran Into Owen Wilson on Cahuenga, and Other Encounters with People Who Don't Know Me" previously published at *The Nervous Breakdown*. Meg Tuite's "Root People" previously published at *The Nervous Breakdown*.

www.unknowneverything.com
ISBN 978-0-9963526-3-5

Contents

Dedicated to the first egg that inexplicably exploded in my hands while I was making breakfast, but NOT to the second egg that exploded later that same day, splattering itself all over my shirt and face at the grocery store, because the second egg made the story too unbelievable.

It's never happened before or since.

—Aaron Dietz

Foreword

These are the stories we want to share with you, in case we die. And it's good that we're sharing them, because science tells us that it's likely we are (eventually) going to die. It's practically inevitable.

And it would be the worst to die without telling these stories because these are the outliers of experience. The ones textbooks don't tell us about. The ones that don't happen often enough for science to even study effectively (so far).

But these things happen, and when they happen they help us become aware that the universe is a far, far more interesting place than our textbooks have led us to believe. The drudgery you may feel from time to time in your daily life could be interrupted at any moment by something truly mysterious that you cannot explain. You never know when it'll happen. And judging by the number of submissions we received and the number of stories we've listened to in dark corners of bars and in side rooms of obnoxious cocktail parties, we would venture to guess that you have a story as well. We hope you tell it.

This book was inspired by Aaron Dietz's *In Case I Die*, a mini-memoir of all the unexplainable things that have happened to him. But the book didn't go far enough. Dietz has an interesting habit of asking others at any opportune moment, "What is the strangest thing that has ever happened to you?" And given the vast number of incredible responses, it was clear that a book was needed to start sharing the stories of everyone.

And so, here we are.

In this book, you'll read about ghosts and UFO's, sure. But you'll also read about people who are taking what we consider "the ordinary" and making it magical, mysterious, or at the least, a captivating puzzle.

Some of these tales are long-kept secrets, only now finding their way into the hands of the public, even as their authors cringe at the thought of their family reading their submission. Other stories in this anthology are not secret but they still need to be told more often.

We mean to start this conversation on a wide scale. Because the worst thing we can do as humans would be to continue to perpetuate the idea that the world is as normal as most mainstream media would have us believe.

—Aaron Dietz and Bud Smith

UFO

Sean Beaudoin

Vodka was involved. I'll admit that from the outset. A half-liter of Popov that had been in my parent's liquor cabinet since 1966. But I swiped it because there was a dance in the school gym, and we needed lube to press ourselves against sweaty girls to the strains of "Hungry Like the Wolf" and "Heat of the Moment." There were some moments. There was some heat. But after a while, Adam and I were like "fuck this," in that utterly liberating way which implies *Even though we are merely sixteen, we recognize the essential falsehood of the premise of The Dance, the fraudulent social interplay, the sexual pandering, the repressively fluorescent lighting—and we intellectually reject it. Mainly in favor of going outside for more vodka.*

The bottle was hidden in the back of my mom's Impala station wagon. We grabbed it and walked down to the football field, big and dark and empty, sat in the bleachers, swigged, bitched, broke down various slights and flirtations. This girl, that girl. This asshole, that asshole. Our friend Mike was supposed to meet us, but never showed. Adam figured it was because his car broke down again, a piss-yellow '71 VW Beetle Mike had bought for three hundred bucks from that waitress with the stringy hair rumored to offer tug jobs in the dry goods closet to enterprisingly handsome busboys. For some reason, we called his car The Veeter. Aside from often not running, The Veeter had problems. Like, you couldn't turn the heat off. Ever. In the middle of August the thing was still a blast furnace, molten air constantly forced through the dash. We kept cardboard in the back seat to cover our bare legs with. The Veeter also had a very distinct sound. A combination of resigned fart and beerhall oohmpah that could be heard at great distances. If it was coming, we always knew.

So we sat in the bleachers, laughed and drank as traffic raced down off the highway. There was a long, looping exit right next to the football field. Cars regularly misjudged the curve, failed to allow sufficient breaking speed and then fishtailed in a panicky slide right up to the stop light. It's amazing there wasn't a fiery Pinto-involved crash three times a day. Or maybe there was, because years later the town dug that shit up and hired someone who could chart a parabola on a napkin before laying down new pavement. Anyway, the exit was mostly quiet until we heard an unmistakable high-Veeter whine roaring in the slow lane. Mike was gonna make it after all. Adam and I slapped five. I took a double-swig of vodka, calculating how much I'd have to drink now plus how much we'd have to apportion to Mike later minus the blood/booze level needed to face a return to the gym, not to mention another round of grindy bumping with Donna Templeton.

"He better slow down," Adam said, as The Veeter approached the exit at speed, carved the turn, released a long tiny *blaaaat*, dropped two gears, backfired, and then...went completely silent.

We watched as it reached the stoplight, but didn't stop. It accelerated and lifted instead, rising two feet.

And then six.

And then ten.

It hovered over the intersection, rose above the pines, and eased out past the 50 yard line, making no sound at all. We made no sound at all. That VW Beetle turned into a balloon that was not a balloon, a helicopter that was not a helicopter. It was a craft of some sort, certainly, because the headlights never turned off. They continued to shine dual spots down onto the field and into the trees, as if searching for something. We ducked while the lights swept over our heads. The Veeter slowed, turned three hundred and sixty degrees high in the air, glided through the parking lot, paused again as if unsure of itself, and then disappeared over the other side of the school. Completely soundless. A gentle apparition.

Adam and I looked at each other, and then looked at the bottle, and then looked at the dark parking lot, but there was nothing to say. Besides a quiet and vaguely terrified "holy shit." Except it was more like he'd go *holyshitholyshitholyshitholyshitholyshit* and I'd go *IknowIknowIknowIknowIknowIknow*.

The next day I saw Mike at work and asked him what happened and he said his car was broke so he stayed home and went to bed early. When I told him what Adam and I saw, he shrugged and went back to the kitchen to talk to the waitress with stringy hair.

Well, that was almost thirty years ago. I've told very few people this story, mainly because it sounds like pure bullshit, or at least some easily explainable fluke that we were too young and dumb to factor in or account for. And also because I have no interest in hearing anyone else's mystical experiences or crazy dreams, which this kind of tale invariably encourages. I do not believe your story, but I attest that mine is completely true and happened exactly as described. I was sixteen and buzzed, but not drunk and definitely not hallucinatory. Adam now lives in deepest Maine and refuses to own, let alone operate, a computer. I am connected, albeit suspiciously. We were spectators to an event with zero precedent in the annals of logic, physics, or gravity. A car came off the highway, full of light and momentum and distinctive engine sounds, and then turned down an exit ramp before silently rising up into the sky and floating away.

I saw it.

Adam saw it.

Fuck you.

Caroline's Visitor

Julie Allen

I shared a duplex with my best friend Sarah and her husband John. My boyfriend, Todd, and I were at their place many nights throughout the week, as we'd party quite a bit back in those days. We were young, in our 20's, and still had energy to last for days on end.

There were some nights when we'd hit it pretty hard. Sarah and John could drink anyone under the table. After a couple 12 packs or hard alcohol on some nights, they'd pass out and wake up and do it again the next day. They were machines. That is, until Caroline came along.

Caroline was their beautiful bouncing, blue eyed bundle of joy. The one thing that made them slow down and become responsible adults. It was a good thing, because many nights we'd have to put them to bed and make sure they were turned to the side, just in case they'd throw up in the middle of the night and drown on their own puke. It wasn't pretty. After having taken care of them so many times in their drunken past and being their best friends, they asked Todd and I to be Caroline's Godparents. We were honored and gladly accepted.

One night at their place, Sarah and John told us an odd story. They said that on several occasions after partying during their wild stage in life, they were awoken to the sound of a woman's voice yelling at them to "Get up!" At first they'd laugh it off thinking it was just a coincidence that they both heard this voice. Until it happened again, and then again. It happened a hand full of times. Needless to say, this story scared me. I lived right next door in the other duplex. I sure didn't want whatever was hanging around on their side, to float over to my side of the duplex and yell at me, too! After a while, I forgot about it. I forgot until one night when Sarah and John had a party and Todd and I were left to take care of baby Caroline.

It had been months since Sarah and John had gotten extremely loaded. I figured they were due. They had been so good since the baby was born, why not cut lose one night and have a good time! They decided to have a cookout and invite all their friends to celebrate the 4th of July. There was booze, pot, and who knows what else everyone was doing. It was a pretty crazy night. Todd and I promised to look after Caroline upstairs while they had a good time with friends. The party lasted until early in the morning when finally everyone went home.

Sarah and John went upstairs to bed and Todd and I made our camp downstairs with sleeping bags. I went up one last time to check on baby Caroline and she was still sleeping soundly, all snuggled in her crib. I checked on Sarah and John and they were out like a light, snoring, and seemed rather peaceful. I went back downstairs and Todd and I went to sleep.

Around 4am, I woke up because I felt hot air on my back. I rolled over from Todd's side, and saw that the sliding glass door was open in the dining room. I thought that was odd because I remember locking down the house after everyone left. I got up and pulled it closed, and lied back down to go to sleep.

Not long after I lied back down, I heard the sound of Caroline cooing. I smiled to myself and thought I'd go up to check on her, when all of a sudden, I heard a woman's voice, too. Sarah must have gotten up to check on Caroline, I thought. Good, I could go back to sleep because I was tired form babysitting all night. After a while of lying there, I heard a soft giggle that sounded unfamiliar to me. I sat up quickly and turned toward the stairs to listen. I thought, could someone have gotten in when the door was open? I continued to sit there, about to wake Todd up. The voice would stop, then start again in a sweet, playful way, with Caroline cooing and making spit noises all the while. Suddenly, Todd whispered, "Do you hear that too?"

I grabbed his shoulder and I whispered, "Yes!"

We sat straight up for a minute, listening to the muffled sound of a lady's voice and our goddaughter, obviously entertained. There was no sound from Sarah or John. After we shook off our shock, we crept quietly up the stairs, not to disturb whoever was up there, when suddenly the lady's voice stopped. We looked at each other and continued normally up the stairs as we would barge in on whoever was up there.

Walking into Caroline's room, Todd flipped on the light. Caroline's little hands rubbed her eyes from the light, but she had been awake. Grabbing her toes, smiling, cooing with goo's and gahs and all drooly faced, she smiled at us. She was alone. There was no sign of anyone. I checked on Sarah and Todd. Still snoring and sound asleep.

Todd's hands were on his hips like he does when he just can't figure something out and we looked at one another and then back at Caroline. We were sober and we both heard the same thing. We didn't say anything, but just looked at Caroline. We took turns holding her, wanting her to tell us who came to visit her, if anyone at all. She just goo-gooed and gah-gahed and smiled. We sat in her room until the sun came up.

The Friendly Fern

Maura O'Connell

Back in the mid-1990s, I was hiking with my sister on Mount Olomana, on the island of Oahu, Hawaii. The mountainside was beautiful and verdant, with large trees and lots of ferns. My sister had gotten ahead of me, so I walked alone for a bit. A cooling breeze had come up, which I welcomed.

I approached a grove of ferns under a huge tree. All of the ferns had been pushed back by the breeze and were lying flat; with one exception. One of the ferns seemed to have been caught in an air current. It was upright and flapping back and forth like a windshield wiper. I laughed because it seemed like it was waving at me. I was in a whimsical mood, so I waved back.

"Hello," I said. The fern kept flapping merrily.

Then I said, "Yes, I see you."

The fern immediately stopped flapping and stood upright for a split second. Then, it slowly lay backward, flattening into the rest of the ferns that were still being pushed by the breeze. I couldn't believe what I saw and ran to catch up with my sister.

"A fern just waved to me!" I exclaimed.

"Oh, that happens all the time up here," she replied, completely unimpressed. My sister lives in Hawaii and often hikes this mountain.

Her comment amazed me. So, waving leaves were commonplace? *Wow, Hawaii truly is magical,* I thought. I lived in Hawaii in the 70s, and I have been back to visit at least 25 times since I moved away. But I have never had another experience like that one.

Old Caples, By the Shoreline

Allie Marini

When I was an undergraduate student at New College, I had an experience at one of the bayside-facing sections of campus that was formerly part of the John & Mable Ringling estate. Old Caples Hall used to be the servants quarters and stable of the Ringling estate, and the borders of the property ended at the white breakers of the bay. The paved corridor leading to the arched entryway to the main building was studded with satsuma and kumquat trees, and the grounds were calm and lovely in daylight, all sparkling turquoise water and painted sunsets scattered across the shoreline. But once the sun sunk down into the water, Old Caples transformed into something decidedly different. After sunset, the building and its grounds seemed to shrink and contract, unsettling the very air surrounding you. Even the carelessly stupid and the haphazardly drunk judiciously avoided Old Caples after sundown. The building and its grounds felt as muggy and sweaty, as oppressive as Florida's humidity in the throes of August.

There were stories, but not about Old Caples: There was Pei Dorm 301, which was always cold, even when no one was running the air conditioner. They said that in 1982, whoever lived there had been fucking around with a Ouija board, conjured something into the room, and it convinced them to kill themselves. And even though no one could remember who they were or what their name was, the fact of the matter was that no student had stayed in Pei 301 for more than a week since 1982, and a lot of them had never even heard the stories until after they'd requested a room transfer. There was also the throne down by the bay, constructed by a student whose name and year had been erased with each telling of the story: supposedly, the student had cracked under the pressure of an unfinished thesis project. The throne was just one piece of a planned installation that never came to pass. The dark streaks on the throne were rumored to be from the thesis student, who set himself on fire while looking out over the Gulf waters one last time. But there weren't any stories about Old Caples. Whatever it was that made the air wrap around you down by the side of its bay, it was something that no one wanted to whisper about, or dream up a story to accompany. No one wanted to be there after dark, and no one wanted to talk about why, just in case talking about it invited it to stay.

My second year at school, I had a film noir class that met weekly at Old Caples and let out at 8:30 p.m. Because I didn't have a car, the easiest way back to my dorm was cutting through the back grounds of Old Caples that ran parallel to the bay and jumping the fence at Cà d'Zan. Once I was over the fence, it was a straight shot across the other side of campus from the unfenced walkway connecting the museum grounds to College Hall. I made this trip once a week for half a semester, and before long, I'd even stopped registering the weird quiet that rolled over the tall seagrass and chain link fence next to the lone picnic table out back.

One evening after class let out, I stopped there to sit down and light a cigarette before hopping the fence and making my way back to my dorm. It was November, and the sky was dark and thick as midnight by the time the sun dipped below the skyline. From the bench of the picnic table, I could see the weird greenlit glow of the Sarasota Quay on the other side of the waters—dark and blooming, like phosphorescent plankton riding the surf. The bay breeze was just strong enough to tamp out the lick of fire from my lighter. As I cupped my hand around the flame, re-lighting my smoke, I registered the distinct feeling of motion in my peripheral vision. A moment later, the wood and load of the picnic bench flexed, as though bearing the weight of another body. Thinking it was someone from class who cut through the back of Caples too, I turned to greet them and offer them a light.

The bench was empty beside me, washed out wood pale under the faded moon in the sky and the faraway glow of streetlights. My smoke coiled around the empty space where I thought I would turn to see shoulders and a face. There was no one to greet. The only sound was the faint slapping of the tide against the stones buttressing the edge of the grounds. The only weight bearing down on the wooden bench beneath my thighs was my own. In the moment before it registered that no one was there or ever had been, I thought they pulled back under the palm tree and stepped into the shadows, watching me. Smoke spooled between my fingertips. I felt the buzz of blood rushing to my ears, a rhythmic rush like a rising tide against a wall of concrete. My visitor slipped back into the shadows, unstoried, except for this.

I Ran Into Owen Wilson on Cahuenga, and Other Encounters with People Who Don't Know Me

Ben Loory

I.

I ran into Owen Wilson on Cahuenga.
Owen Wilson, I said, stopping short.
Hey man, he said, how's it going? Are there are a lot of cops around here?

Cops? I said.
I was kind of concerned.
Like, what do you mean? I said.
Cops, he said. You know, police. I don't know if I can park my car here.

I turned and looked and Owen Wilson's car was parked right in the middle of the sidewalk.

Oh, I said. Well, I don't know. I mean, I wouldn't do that.

No? he said.
He looked at the car.
I won't be very long, he said.
Well, I said. I don't know. I just wouldn't, is all.

But in the end Owen Wilson didn't listen.
Thanks, man, he said to me.
It's okay, I said. I hope you don't get towed.
Me too, he said, and walked away.

I don't know what happened to Owen Wilson's car.
It was a red car. I don't remember what kind.
A few days later I heard he'd tried to kill himself.
But I guess everything worked out fine.

II.

I saw Forest Whitaker driving on Franklin. He cut me off in a big SUV.
Fuck you! I yelled, and sped up to catch him.
I hadn't seen who was driving.
Then I did.

Oh, I said, Forest Whitaker.
He had that funny eye, you know.
I don't remember which eye it was.
I remember thinking, Maybe he can't see so well.

I used to be in a band where the drummer wore an eye patch. He'd lost an eye in a car accident. He'd had a lot of facial reconstructive surgery. He looked like Sammy Davis Jr., which was funny. (He was a white guy.)

Maybe it's a thing about one-eyed people that makes them really bad drivers. I mean obviously there's the depth perception thing. But maybe there's also something else. Maybe it's an angry-at-the-world thing that happens. Takes over. Makes you wanna kill people. But really, our drummer was always very nice. So Forest Whitaker was probably just an asshole.

III.

One day I went to Barney's and bought a shirt. Don't ask me what I was doing. $750 dollars for a shirt? Okay, actually I found a cheap one.

Anyway, I was standing there in line—it was a big line, there was only one cashier—and suddenly I noticed that Spock was in front of me.
Wow, it's Spock! I said.

When I say I said it, I mean in my head, because he didn't hear me or anything. He was standing there with a whole bunch of shirts on his arm.
His were the thousand dollar ones.

Anyway, we stood there and stood there and stood there. There was something with the guy at the front. He didn't know how to work his wallet or something. I didn't care—it was like I was Spock's friend!

Spock was pretty old and his ears weren't pointy.

Leonard Nee-moy, I thought, trying it out.
It was weird to say his real name and not just Spock.
Then I heard a voice calling out.

I can help one of you over here! the voice said.
It was a cashier at a register to the side. There was no
one in line. There was no wait at all.
Spock looked at me. I looked at him.

I moved first. I admit it, I'm an asshole. I'm the
Forest Whitaker in this story. I skipped away with
my one cheap shirt.
Then I laughed at Spock inside my head.

When I tell this story to people they smile.
Weren't you worried about the Vulcan neck pinch?
they say.
But to tell you the truth, it never crossed my mind.
It was just Leonard Nimoy; Spock's pretend.

IV.

I saw Robin Williams at the Virgin Megastore. He
was looking at the DVD new releases. I was standing
on the other side and I looked up. I saw him. And I
saw him see me.

Let me be clear: Robin Williams looked like shit.
I love Robin Williams, but he did. He was skinny
and unshaven and his skin was almost gray. He was
wearing an old army jacket.

The worst thing about it was he looked so sad.
Robin Williams! I wanted to say. You're so funny!

But he didn't look funny. He didn't, at all. He looked like he might crumble away.
For a minute I just stood there and tried to decide how to go about saving Robin Williams's life.
Maybe I could buy him an omelet or something, I thought.
I couldn't think of anything else.

But then it was over. Robin Williams walked away. He walked slowly, casually—he was scared. I knew that he was trying to get away from me.
He was in the corner where the video games were.

I knew that Robin Williams wasn't buying video games. His hands were in his pockets and he was old. I mean, I'm old and he's older than me. We're lucky they allow us in the store.

I stood there for a while, while he let off this vibe that said PLEASE GET THE FUCK AWAY FROM ME. I guess he just wanted to be left alone so he could wander around town looking glum.

And so in the end I turned away, bought my CDs, and went out to the car.
On the way home I started to cry.
If Robin Williams can't be happy, how can I?

V.

One night really late I went down to Ralph's. This was when I lived up in West Hollywood. I had my loaf of bread, my diet Coke, a bunch of Slim Jims.
I got in line behind a beautiful woman.

I don't know where the guy is, she said.
The cashier guy wasn't there. No one was.
He'll probably be back, I said. He can't be far.
Then I got a better look at her.

Hey, I said. Do I know you? You look really familiar.
Yeah, she said, I get that a lot.
Then I realized.
Demi Moore.

Demi Moore, I thought. What's she doing here? At
Ralph's in Hollywood at 3 a.m.?
This was back when she and Bruce Willis were
together.
I looked around, but I didn't see him.

This is crazy, she said. I've been here forever. And all
I'm trying to buy is this.
She held up an Evian bottle and waved it a little.
I smiled to be nice and shook my head.

If you want, I said, suddenly having an idea, give me
the money and I'll pay for it when he gets back.
Are you sure? she said. That's really very nice.
It's okay, I said. I don't mind.

And so Demi Moore gave me a five, and walked on
out into the night. And I stood there a while until the
cashier came back, and I paid for my own stuff and
kept the five.

Floating Light Bulb

Pei Yu Lin

When I was little, I was really afraid of the dark. We lived in a house with a detached bathroom three minutes' walk away from the main house. When I needed to go to the bathroom in the middle of the night, my mom would always hold my hand and take me to the bathroom in pitch black darkness.

One night, while I was sitting on the toilet holding my mom's hand, I saw a glowing light bulb floating in the air, and I thought that was really nice that it wasn't so dark anymore.

I asked my mom, "Why is there a light bulb glowing in mid-air?" She said she didn't know.

I then asked her if that was normal, and she said yes.

I never saw that glowing light bulb again but I am not that afraid of the dark anymore, especially when I am at home.

When the Thaw Comes

Erin Parker

for S.

Six months after life pulled the rug out from under me, I decide to run away from the suburbs of Los Angeles and go back to school in a safer, slower world. Safer is more important than slower, but slower is appealing. I long for my old out of state college in the foothills of the Wasatch Front. I want the red canyons of Color Country. I want mountains covered with quaking aspen and bristlecone pine. I want to throw myself into Lit classes, to write papers about words and stories and their meaning. I want time to move differently than it does in Los Angeles.

I register for classes over the phone, pack a few boxes and give notice at my job. And then with a week until classes start and no place to live, I leave the crisp sunny days of Southern California in January, drive for hours through the desert, and arrive in the muddy gray of a winter that's gone on too long. I have reserved three nights in a motel on

Main Street, confident I'll find a furnished room to rent. I will rent a room where I can find my way out of the dark. There is no plan B. And here it is: a room for rent listed on the first flyer on the first bulletin board at the Student Center on campus. I take the flyer down and drive carefully on icy roads to the address. I knock on the front door of the house. The woman who answers tells me the room for rent is in a three bedroom apartment in their basement, and two of the rooms have tenants. She leads me to the driveway lined with snow drifts, down some dark stairs next to the garage, and knocks on the door. A girl about my age lets us in. Inside it's a cozy, dim, wood-paneled basement and the bedrooms have windows right under the ceiling with dirty snow piled against the glass panes outside.

The bedroom for rent is in the back of the basement apartment, and when she opens the door of the room, nobody says a word. It's musty and dark and could use some paint, but it's quiet and furnished and that's all I want.

"I'll take it," I say, turning to the owner and the two girls who live there. My new roommates are Viv and Tina. They exchange a glance and smile at me.

The winter progresses and the snow gets higher until the windows are covered with gray and no light gets through the ice. I live underground like a rabbit. I listen to records and read books and drink hot peppermint tea against the cold. Sometimes I stay up late and write stories in a notebook. I sporadically attend classes. I eat Top Ramen and hardboiled eggs because they are cheap. Sometimes my roommates make chocolate chip cookies and invite people from church to come over and play Uno. I realize fairly quickly I may have made a mistake in coming back to this town. Everything has slowed down and has now overwhelmed me. I feel buried in this underground room with no light. Paralysis has set in. I am homesick for things I can't put into words.

One night I have trouble going to sleep and am lying in the dark looking up at the ceiling. I am wondering how to gather the energy I would need to move back home. The thought of packing my car up and driving home feels impossibly difficult. The heavy air in the room becomes heavier and the dark gets darker. Over by the closet there's a ripple in the shadows, and maybe it's from the tree branches outside through the ice on the windows, but maybe it's not. I sit up in bed, straining to see into the corner across the room. I realize I am not alone, and go cold.

A girl's face flashes lightning-quick into my mind, and I see her shaking her head at me, disappointed and a little amused. In an instant, I see myself like she sees me: a girl huddled in bed, drowning in self-pity and circles. I see her face again, like quick frames from a film. She's shaking her head, a mocking half-smile on her lips. She's chiding me. She can't believe the despair I have allowed myself to fall into.

"You have everything," she says to me, her words flashing in my mind. She's not sympathetic, or wise, or all knowing. She is annoyed. This is something you might say to a friend who needs to be told the hard truth. A friend who has taken things too far for too long, and could benefit from a reminder to get up and start living. I have a strong impression of a finger wagging. Enough, she scolds. *Enough.*

"Stop feeling sorry for yourself," she says. "You're *alive*, so you have *everything*."

She's in front of the closet door facing me, laughing a little, shaking her head, mouth pursed in amusement. I strain to see her in the dark. I feel her looking at me. She's right there. *Is* someone there? Curiosity wins out over fear. For a moment I am comfortable, content even, accepting that I may have gently slid sideways and lost my grip on reality. I am surprised it's so easy. I reach for the lamp on my nightstand and before I can switch it on, she's gone. She's just gone. I'm still in the dark, but very much alone.

I wrap the covers tight around me and lie back down, holding this flash of a girl in my mind. The impression of her words, her knowing look, her message that is starting to make sense. Or maybe I am losing it. Have already lost it. I am kind of okay with that as I drift off to sleep.

The next morning I wake up feeling better than I have in weeks. The snow is almost gone now and I can see light out the windows. Spring must be close. I breathe deeply and smile, lighter and happier than I have been in a long time. Maybe I am crazy, but crazy feels pretty good.

In the afternoon, my roommates and I are in the living room doing homework with the radio on. I'm drinking hot tea. Perhaps we will make cookies later.

"You're in a good mood today," says Tina.

"The weirdest thing happened," I say. "Last night I couldn't sleep. Then, you know how you can feel that someone is in the room with you? Well, that's what I felt. Like someone was in my room. I got this image in my head of this girl. She was in my room over by the closet. She was kind of making fun of me for being so depressed."

They look at each other quickly.

"What," I say. "You think I'm crazy. I know it sounds weird."

"No it doesn't," Viv says.

"It was like this girl was telling me to stop feeling sorry for myself," I continue slowly, "that I have no excuse to feel depressed. She said I was alive, so I had everything, that I was lucky. I mean, that makes sense, right?"

They look at each other again, and Tina says to Viv, "Should we tell her?"

My heart starts pounding and I'm filled with apprehension. "Tell me what."

"Didn't you ever wonder," Viv says slowly, "why your room was available when you moved here to start school in the middle of the year? Nobody has lived in that room for a long time. Nobody wanted to."

"I just thought I got lucky when I found the ad that the room was available," I say. "But you're right, it is kind of odd."

"There was a girl that lived in your room about a year and half ago," Viv says, her eyes filling. "She died. She had left to go to her hometown, but never made it. She disappeared. She was missing for a couple of weeks. Then they found her body. She was murdered. It was an awful time, such a nightmare." She stops and looks at me, wiping her eyes. "This is hard to talk about. You would have liked her."

Viv is crying now, remembering, telling me how the girl's dad and brothers showed up. How she helped them pack up boxes, clean the bedroom and load their car up with her things. How she had always kept the door to the bedroom closed, and sometimes she would hear sounds in the room, like someone was opening the desk drawer. Sometimes she would find the light in the closet on even though no one had been in there. The older couple who owned the house didn't try to rent the basement bedroom out for over a year. They'd put the notice up at the Student Center the week before I got into town and came by. There had been no interest until I showed up.

Tina jumps in. "I didn't live here last year," she says, "so I didn't know her. But I knew the story, and poor Viv was trying to deal with everything that happened. Nobody else wanted to live here. So when you showed up to look at the room, we decided not to tell you. You looked so nice, we didn't want to scare you away. I am sorry."

Viv wipes her eyes and says with a sad smile, "I hope you don't want to move out now."

I am letting it all sink in. Now there is this girl who has died a horrible death. This girl who was my age, who had slept in the same room, under the same iced windows, and in the same bed. This girl who had lost her life, who saw me wasting mine by feeling sorry for myself. This girl who told me I had my whole life in front of me. Who knows when it will all be over? None of us know. She hadn't known. She told me to wake up, to grab life, to make it what I wanted and stop wasting time. Because even the bad times mean you're alive. And when you're alive, you do have everything. She was telling me to get up, seize it and hold on tight. Because it is beautiful and rich and far, far too short. She told me to start living.

And so I did.

Manic: In Case of My Disappearance

Heather Dorn

Sometimes I am magic.

Of course, I know I can't really be magic. I'm a fairly logical person. I believe in evolution, consider myself an atheist, in my last year of my PhD studies. But sometimes I do become magic. Even though I probably do not.

People think Bipolar means that you're happy one minute and sad the next, but the cycles last much longer than a moment, sometimes weeks or more, and happy and sad don't in any way describe the highs and lows or their severity.

Mania's lies are beautiful and violent. It can feel like a dream where I physically change and take on a separate and different body. I become some Ms.

Hyde version of myself. I look thinner, my eyes blaze, I'm hilarious, my hands stop shaking. Everything is warmer, colors are rich and things stand out in ways that I don't notice other days. The tree in the front yard looks menacing and I wonder if it's a threat. I think the people three tables over must be saying they like my dress. I can hear them because I'm magic.

My lamp looks so yellow it's like neon popping toward me 3-D. I think I might be the best person to ever play the game of Survivor—as soon as they accept me. My thoughts are fast. They shoot through my mind too fast to catch. But when I do catch an idea, I believe it to be brilliant.

I only believe in magic when I'm manic and only I can do it. When I'm manic, I can use my eyes to melt someone into me. I don't know how this works, but I've seen it work on shes sitting at bars. Lashes down, then up. And I look at her and she knows I'm her new best friend and we talk until closing. Lashes down, then up for hes I want to buy another pair of jeans from me. Smile. It doesn't have to be sincere. Just interesting or beneficial to me. I don't feel emotions like guilt, just want. I flutter my lashes at my husband for four or five days in bed until another cycle washes me semi-stable again.

But I also explode things.

When I'm manic, I can explode whole relationships with very little thought. Mania is something like adrenaline and I want to destroy everything like a hurricane and I'm just as effective. But when everything is broken and the storm passes, I wake up and don't remember.

I remember what happened. I remember what I did. Most of the time. But I don't remember *her*, that person who takes my body. That person who is me and not me. And I wonder how she lives inside of me still, with little warning of when she's coming and what kind of knife she's carrying.

We are magic.

But magic like a god, who can have what she wants at the expense of everyone else. Magic like a child, who can only take and has nothing to give but glinting eyes. Magic like new relationships, where nobody has flaws. That you can see, yet.

And I know that we are crazy. But we are also magic. You can be two things. And maybe the crazy is part of the magic.

When I'm manic, people love me. I decide they will love me and then they do. I talk so easily, make eye contact. I have to make eye contact because that's how the magic works. When I'm manic, I move more quickly. I can twirl around lampposts and run across the street and back in a blur. I'm like a cheetah and I do scratch.

And I know that I'm crazy. But I'm also magic. And maybe the crazy is the magic?

When I'm manic, I become a cheetah.

Once when I was a cheetah, I made a woman melt into me. I made her think I could sing. I made her think I was a sparkle.

Once when I was a cheetah, I ran so fast I compiled a list of 132 authoritative sources in one night on the final female in horror films.

Once when I was a cheetah, I met a woman in a bar who wore braids like a schoolgirl. Ribbons and all. After a beer of conversation, she agreed to dance with me. I remember pulling her braids during "Manic Monday." I don't remember her name. If I could stay manic and alive, she might still be my girlfriend.

And I know that I'm crazy. But I'm also magic.

Untold Story #1

Peg Quinn

I was eighteen, leaving my waitress job in rural Nebraska at 1:30am, speeding down a dirt road on my usual route home.

Suddenly my car was braking hard. Thinking something might have rolled beneath the brake pedal, I tried to look down and maintain control at the same time, panicking, having no idea what could be happening.

I came to a screeching halt as a train roared past, rocking my car. There were no lights or electronic gates to warn drivers.

I sat very still, watching the train, wondering what had happened. I drove slowly home. There weren't any more problems with my car or brakes.

Root People

Meg Tuite

The world expanded when a stranger, who would have slammed back Reverend Jim Jones Kool-Aid without question, asked me if I knew where the molasses was.

"Sugar is the yeast beast," she said. "Only bake with molasses."

This was a gas station with beer, wine, chips, ice cream, tampons, and motor oil. My head moved horizontally. Molasses did not fit into the repertoire until Kool-Aid rounded a corner of a three-aisle gas-stop with a bottle in hand.

I had just moved into a shack in a mining town outside Santa Fe. My existence for over a decade had been parked in downtown Chicago in a high-rise working at advertising firms. Everyone was an addict. Gucci bags with gold tiny spoons were Christmas gifts.

We wore long linen skirts in muted colors, snorted through the most expensive bathroom stalls in the city. It was either leave or die.

After shivering for a week buried under covers with snow filtering through cracks in the split seams of this shed, I decided to put a coat over my pajamas, throw myself in the car, and drive to get some supplies. This was the only store for miles, as far as I knew.

"Are you on vacation?" I asked, as if I was a local.

She set her molasses on the counter and pulled a change purse out of some unseen pocket of her patchwork skirt. "Have you been to the Tibetan stupa on Airport Road?" she asked.

I stared at her. I had actually landed in a place exempt of chit-chat. And Tibetans were here.

"You should come to the chantings on Saturdays. Padmasambhava's mantra will reignite you." I could taste the dust in my teeth when she studied me. I was a gray storm in the distance, whether seen or not, easily forgotten.

I honed in on 'Kool-Aid' eyes. There was potential here to unhinge the scourge of sobriety without snorting or swallowing.

"Have you been to a channeling?" she asked.

The addict in me was reactivated. "No, but I would," I said. "Have you?"

The sunken bulbs of her overcast lids lifted without surprise or thrill. She wasn't one of those converts who puts another gold star in their book each time they lasso another bloodless sack. More like the carnival guy who takes everyone's ticket before they step into a caged egg and straps them in upside down, whether they're ninety, or four years old, with a shrug.

"Friday night Sartorius and Schnikter are going to be here."

"Schnickter?" I could imagine a Sartorius, but a Schnikter had me in drizzly Eastern Europe at a cafe with a bald, shipwreck of a man who'd survived the Holocaust.

"They're coming from Los Lunas." Kool-Aid put her hand over her lips. "I mean, that's not where they live, you know. They stay with friends from up here." When she said, 'up here,' she used air quotations with her index and middle fingers.

I nodded.

'Up here,' only heightened my exuberance. She got out a pen and wrote an address down. "This is where the meeting will be, at six."

"Can you drive?" I asked. Lost in my body of frayed nerves, I barely made it to the homestead less than a mile away, still circumventing whether this backroad life without drugs was going to be a long voyage or a wrong turn.

* * *

Kool-Aid and her stick-shift had no sense of rhythm. We lurched toward a luminous adobe house flickering lights and prayer flags weary from indiscriminate welcoming, jolted to a stop before smacking one of the BMW's packed into a gravel driveway. It was a car lot of Volvos, Mercedes, BMW's without the balloons and a litany of optimistic salesmen, except for one alien Subaru with bumper stickers collaging its backend with 'world peas,' 'kill your TV,' 'God is Green,' dented and aged amidst this nocturnal haze of wealth.

Thirty people circled an open kitchen and living room separated by a bar lathered with food I'd never eaten in my life. One woman walked us through a tour of hors d'oeuvres. Pear and gorgonzola pizza, roasted eggplant in duck sauce, quiche, frittatas, artichoke and lemon fritters, and desserts that made me rethink what kind of empire kept the cosmos in motion. I wished I'd worn the blue peacoat with the fat pockets.

Kool-Aid's body exiled itself into an oppressive container, hunched and scarcely visible, as a round, cramped woman barely over five feet waddled towards us with crumbs framing her lips. "Delusion is no more than illusion," she said. Her dyed hair was definitely a home-job. The roots were black, and a reddish-blonde hue consecrated the bottom half of her stringy hair; one of those wash-your-hair-once-a-week girls.

Kool-Aid put her hands together and bowed.

The pseudo-blonde dismissed her and turned her gaze on me, giving me a grainy windshield swipe of a haunting. "Your chakras are clogged. Lazaria does colonics. Make an appointment."

Lazaria walked toward me with card in hand. She was thin as a bottle, skin stretched like a drum. "You have sex with cookies, eh?" she asked in either a Polish or Russian accent. "Take card. We open gate, clear out acres of you." Her make-up was its own landscape. She patted my rotting intestines, shook her head at the loaded pile of food on my paper plate and sashayed away.

A woman clapped her hands. Scripted as a fire drill, flowing, gilded women and men sat in a semi-circle on the carpet around the kitchen, while the squat blonde and a guy, not much taller than her, with a beige mullet tufted on his head in a high-five, stood before us.

The hostess, a woman with a debased smile that licked any version of happiness raw, seemed more afraid of life than I was. She must have had one of those punchcards, *ten colonics and the next one's free*, a regular of Lazaria's. All elbows, cheekbones, and hollow where a body should have been. "We are most humbled and honored to welcome Sartorius and Schnikter who have come a long, long way to connect with us." The woman lowered her scoliotic spine, dropped her shrunken head and limped off stage right.

Kool-Aid had tears in her eyes, clapped zealously with the group and hugged me. My armpits emanated gorgonzola-pickled terror. I held my head in my hand so it wouldn't tremor.

Sartorius raised her dimpled, waffling arms up and out. She may have been short, but she was no Lady Finger. She was a bagel in a violet mumu.

"We come from Earth's inner core. Human contamination leeches into the crevices where we reside." The bulk of Sartorius sifting through any crevice was hard to envision. Schnikter kept nodding his overly-bleached head. "We have been called up to speak of the end. Water is a gift, not an absolute."

I'm guessing S & S didn't have a landline. I looked around the room. None of these people gave a shit about water. They were definitely golfers, every one of them. Golf courses in the desert were as rampant as souvenir shops selling turquoise bear and turtle fetishes, dusty bags of red chile. I'd taken a few road trips over the years. It took a blast of Niagara Falls every day to keep those greens as emerald as they were. Juniper, cacti, tumbleweed and arroyos, splash a few elm trees and Russian olives here and there for the exotic effect, and that was the cracked and weathered sigh of inertia that echoed its lack in clumps between bald spaces.

We listened to our dismal destiny ahead. California, Texas, and New Mexico ravaged by droughts until no human could exist: temperatures rising, water evaporating; flattened by tornadoes, hurricanes, earthquakes, recessions and wars, hate crimes and pollution. Sartorius and Schnikter took turns flaunting disasters or staring ominously at us. When one of them dead-eyed me, I had to use both hands to hold my head steady.

People raised their hands. We were back in grade school.

This could have been doctors and golfers anonymous.

"I'm a doctor," said one, rattling off statistics on the significant increase of breast cancer. S & S nodded, raised blonde eyebrows letting us know this had been foreknowledge.

"Yes," another doctor said foraging more statistics on ovarian cancer.

And then another and another: gynecologist, plastic surgeon, chiropractor, acupuncturist all waving arms as a merry-go-round of cancer and birth defects erupted like abscessed marriages throughout their waiting rooms.

A few people wanted information on investments they'd made.

Another wanted to know if her suicided daughter had a message.

A couple had an autistic boy who only played with blue toys. "What did blue mean? He gnaws on food but won't swallow it. His tongue clicks when his cheeks are filled like a chipmunk. Should we worry?" they asked.

Sartorius and Schnikter were fierce sonars as they answered questions, their conviction infallible like two dogs' genitals sucked together in coitus.

I blanked out much of what they said. I focused on breathing. When closed in by bodies, I forgot to inhale, shook more visibly. I saw mirrors with lines of coke. Heard the melodious staccato of razorblades slicing through powder on glass. The few times I navigated in on S & S backlit by the kitchen bar, they merged into one of those lunatic dolls from a horror film or creatures with lizard-tongued lassoes shooting in and out.

Did I wash these jeans? A chance of salvaging a tinfoil treasure of white dust clinging like lint was possible. I stuck my fingers in the front pockets and searched desperately, imagined someone behind me wondering if I was masturbating. My notebook was open in my lap. If I could sniff one pinkie-full, I'd be aggressive and absurd as the sun. The few questions I had scribbled in my cabin before the gathering would be asked.

1. Do you think there's a connection between dinosaurs zapped off the planet and an increase in architects and high-rises?

2. What is it about the past that persists on doubting itself into the present?

3. If there's reincarnation, why can't we just kill someone who isn't making the cut in this life without being held accountable?

4. How come drugs are illegal?

I couldn't look at my notebook, let alone talk. Yes, I had somehow infiltrated this room permeated with my vision of the illuminati, but why did this experience arrive at the same time I was saturated with terror, under attack from my body that craved to go fetal?

Schnikter detached himself from what was happening and pointed at me. "Drugs are contrived antennae. Your revelations are merely static, nothing more."

He could see my toxic interior. Holy shit! I put my quivering pen to page and started writing.

"We are Root people, live with a community in the middle of the Earth. We eat roots, have no need for sunlight. You can survive on what propagates around you. Grocery stores and processed food have deluded generations into torturing land. Human hands supply you and will ultimately destroy you."

I recompassed this pudgy couple. It made sense that they had tree-trunk-hued hair roots. But, how could squishy, flabby bodies live on tuberous stalks alone? Many of the women around me were either anorexic or bulimic, evoked images of deprivation and sucking on celery, unlike this couple who appeared no different than anyone else raking their way through Burger King, Wendy's, Dunkin Donuts, and McDonalds before they blasted back to their loathsome lack of light and flavor.

* * *

Five years later, Mom moved out to Santa Fe to die. She had ovarian cancer. I lived with her, sat by her bed with a notebook. Writing was an intoxication and much cheaper than drugs. Documenting time was less painful than watching the clock. When Mom's eyes opened, the tedium and stench of existence dissolved into stories.

"Spent the afternoon with the boys," she said.

"Do I know them?" I asked.

"The pompous bastards believe anyone who doesn't know them is an idiot."

"What did they say?"

"The usual crap men spew on and on about themselves."

Mom had a bad marriage. "Like what?" I asked.

"Who made the biggest impact on the world. Dead and still fighting."

This sounded good.

"Socrates and Plato. Heard of those boys? Isn't it enough that people study, read their work? They're all still in the sandbox," Mom said.

I wrote everything she said in my notebook. Mom saw Emily Dickinson and Don Quixote, William Faulkner and Thomas Wolfe.

"You know, Wolfe, right?" she asked. "He couldn't keep his hands off his package when he was writing. The top of the refrigerator was his desk. He was 6'5, wrote those beauties while ransacking his own goods. Quite an accomplishment."

Mom was a librarian. Her last days were fused with exceptional writers and characters in the room with her.

When Mom dozed, I passed out in the chair next to her bed.

She'd cough, her eyelids, swollen and yellow would crest us back to a here, whatever here that was.

"Do you want me to make a smoothie?"

"How about coffee and a Whopper?" Mom asked.

"Okay." I got whatever she craved. Burger King was not a stop we'd ever made. Fast food was a rare occurrence like contracting pneumonia or breaking an arm when we were kids. Dad was an opinionated hippie. Mom cooked meat, vegetables and potatoes for five kids and a husband, endless mouths of dusk-devouring lifetimes.

I unwrapped and placed the Whopper on one of her antique pink glass plates when I got back. Mom's collection glowed on shelves to be admired, never used before she got cancer. Meals were all about presentation and smell now. The floating tumors only let food get so far in her system and then she'd vomit.

I made coffee while she examined the specimen. "It's fueled with the pulse of back alleys and fists, can you smell it?" She rotated the burger, held it close to her nose. "Singapore, Malaysia, the Isle of Wight." She stroked the bun. Her fingers were wrinkled and bruised, notched trees. Her eyes scrutinized me, impossibly blue. "I never went anywhere. Books were my only way out."

She caressed the Whopper. "That's it," she said. "The greasy stench of sweet grief. Look at it." She tried to lift the tri-layered monstrosity up to her mouth. Tomatoes, lettuce, onions, pickles, burger patty, and slathering innards of condiments collapsed from her grip, slithered down her nightgown onto the sheets and powder blue bedspread into a bloody massacre. She lifted her hands covered in ketchup and grinned. "Now, that's a crucifixion."

Dying was a renaissance. Mom was silent most of my existence. Vacate burnt its neon sign across her 'knick-knack' features that lined up while she cleaned, grocery shopped, cooked, ironed. The only difference between her and the other mothers on the block was that she read. She didn't discuss the books she'd read, barely commented, yet here was a sharp-tipped, thorned woman of truth propped up in a hospital bed in a stagnant trailer.

My notebook was a mausoleum of Mom's unleashed words. The staccato of pen skating across pages paled beneath the trek of her predictions moving like a train rifling over tracks.

"A repelling place for such a precious group," Mom said, while I was changing her nightgown and sheets, rolling her from side to side as the hospice nurse had shown me, washing the remnants of Burger King off of her with a sponge bath.

I nodded, as if I'd been there.

"The Root People," she said.

I stared at her. It had been years since that night. Weirdness doomed to be forgotten; a castaway with other unresolved, traumatic, and humiliating experiences in those huge, blank cavities of a synaptic-free cortex.

"Root People?" I asked.

"Cordial and inviting, but the food was an abomination. Rats eat better than that," she said.

I never told Mom about that night or any of the others. Drugs, boyfriends with GED's or any 'spasmodic behavior', as she called it, was dismissed when she picked up whatever book she was reading and ignored me.

"Strange," she added. "I don't get how they eat gritty twigs and still gain weight. They're short. They're chunky. They're blondes with bad haircuts. But very knowledgeable." She motioned for the bedpan.

I wedged it in place and left the room.

The window in the kitchen opened out to a back lot of chollas reaching up from barren fields like antlers of dead animals. This was a city of wasted space and withering reflections.

I opened up the notebook and started reading everything she'd said from the beginning.

A Pinhead at Safeway

Steven Gowin

At Safeway last night
I saw a pinhead, a kid with microcephaly.
In microcephaly, the face grows at a normal rate
but the head does not.

I didn't stare,
but when I got home,
I couldn't mention the child.
They would wonder why I brought it up at all.

No one wants to hear about that.
I would have said "pinhead." That's wrong isn't it?
Why even mention it, why be blamed? Still...
Last night, I saw a pinhead at Safeway.

Changing of the Guides

Sarah Sarai

I was asleep, in bed, with my boyfriend. So this was a long time ago—I hadn't come out. It was summer and hot, this being Los Angeles. I woke up, maybe 3am. That sounds about right. The night was fully invested in its identity, its darkness, its quiet. The daylight was somewhere over the East Coast, working up a sweat, struggling with its daily exercise, its impressive need to keep moving west.

There was a noise, small and deceptively insignificant. A car crash outside would not have deceived me. Books or a vase tumbling from a shelf as the cat explored would not have deceived me. But the non-sound, the presence of an almost-sound. What was that?

I sat up as well as I could. The bed was a mattress on the floor. Throwing my legs over the edge didn't have the same meaning it does now that I have one of those towering mattresses the size of a bouncy room on a frame. No, I had to be conscious as I pushed up, set my feet on the bare floor and peered around.

My boyfriend snored less gently than George Harrison's guitar wept. Unless I shook him or shouted, I was, essentially alone. Except I wasn't. I saw that. I very distinctly saw two tiny beings, miniaturized, two "Honey, I shrunk the psychic entities"-presences the size of the King and Queen on a chessboard. They were mobile, as fluid in movement as a human. They were small and alive in their own way.

I understood without second-guessing myself. They were my spirit guides. This was a changing of the guard. The spirit guides I'd had for quite a while—years—were leaving and I was witnessing, either really seeing or really being aware of, my new advisors.

You ask, What's a spirit guide, or, What the Hell? They are sent from the green room we all waited in before birth. They know a thing or two, though some may have more epochs of experience than others. I learned about them when I was combatting a chronic illness (which I kicked, though it took a long time). Every Monday night for two years I attended lectures of Rosalyn Bruyere, a new age specialist and director of the Center for Healing Light in Glendale, California. A scientifically-validated aura reader, Ms. Bruyere was tested at the Department of Kinesiology at the University of California, Los Angeles. Best I can explain the procedure is that a subject—students and patients from the UCLA hospital—was hooked up to a lie detector-type gizmo and then physically manipulated by the kinesthesiologists, PhDs and PhD candidates. Bruyere, also, was hooked up. When Bruyere said she saw blue, the scientists would note where the "needles" registered in the testing equipment. They were always consistent. When Bruyere saw "blue" the graph was at, let's say, a 75 percent slope. Same for the other colors of the aura; they were always consistent so red was always the same slope, as were orange, yellow, green, white, purple. Whether or not she saw "blue" (but she did), she was completely consistent.

She was also consistent and valuable in talking about spirit guides, which a student of psychology might consider an intuition helper, if that student leaned toward a groovy psychology or Jung. They come to us from that mystery closet, the universe. And during anyone's lifetime, he or she will have several pair. And during anyone's lifetime, they can be helped, if they listen. The following Monday in class I asked about what I had seen in the middle of the night. Was it something I'd created or imagined? Bruyere told me to believe what I saw and felt.

I did and I still do. Twenty years later I was sitting in a committee meeting, at a job, in New York City where I now live. A person I'd never met, "Connie," let's call her, sat across from me. And I saw them. Bing! Her spirit guides and my spirit guides greeting each other. One was—and I'm laughing, believe me, I'm laughing, I've beat you to your understandable cynicism—an old bow-legged cowboy eagerly greeting a Chinese sage in an embroidered silk jacket. The size of chess pieces and not really visible. A teeny convocation of astral beings, on the beeline between the woman's and my pate, greeting each other as friends will.

A plausible copout is that even if the specifics of what I saw weren't real, they represented a fictional reality, an allegory. My intuition tells me my experience is real. When I talked to that woman after the meeting, there was a genuine connection surpassing geography or gender. An old-friendness. In September 2001, a few days after the attack, after the Towers fell, I saw my mother, who had passed on a month previous in August 2001. She, no longer alive, was back here in New York, where she was born, helping the dead with their shocking transition. She was 86 when she died. It was coming. She knew that. But the workers in the World Trade Center did not have a clue what was going to happen that day. My mother was a helper-type in life and now in death. When I told friends they said, Believe it.

I've strayed. Or have I. My point is, believe it. What you are thinking or feeling may seem too Rod Serling-y to be real but real and reality are vague and indistinct words. I haven't paid any attention to my spirit guides, now that I'm moving closer to my mother's side of things and they punish me by ignoring me. Or howling. Just last week I was feeling a specific emptiness that comes from not having a current psychic-type practice, a feeling similar to the emptiness I feel when I've ignored my religious beliefs. Are they different? Because I recall supernatural beings and guides all over the Hebrew Bible and the New Testament.

My spirit guides still have advice for me. Quite literally, they are here for me. But I don't know what the newest pair, probably my last, are dolled-up in.

Lights

Tantra Bensko

At the old homestead on Sand Mountain, Alabama, I liked to go regularly for walks at night alone by the creek. At one point the pine needle-covered trail veers away from the creek by a few yards and a small branch angles off. As I was sitting on the little bridge over the branch one warm summer night several years ago, I saw a string of lights coming along the path in the distance.

I didn't know what to do, thought they might be the local animal-sacrificing Satanists that people had been talking about, doing a dark ritual, carrying candles, and I didn't want to draw attention to myself by standing up to leave. I didn't want to jump to conclusions, either, and was curious about what was going on. So I stayed on the bridge, waiting for them to follow the trail to me. At first I was just frozen, frankly, and I worked on emboldening myself to do whatever was needed as they got to where I was. What that might be rushed through my brain faster than the creek water flowed by that night, full from the storm the day before.

Each light was equidistant from the others, as if the people were walking in measured distance from each other, and carrying candles at a comfortable height, yet they must have had someone check them over first, as they were all the same height. What an elaborate performance that must have been, getting the taller people to carry the candles lower. They walked at the same slow pace, and stayed to the center in between the pines, oaks, and walnuts. The moon was crescent, so I couldn't see the people themselves, though as they grew closer, I grew a little surprised the flames didn't illuminate them at all. There were dozens of them, as far as I could see. I heard no sounds of walking. I shivered.

It wasn't the right situation for swamp gas. Fireflies would have flashed off and on, and had a green tinge, had no reason to go along a trail, surely wouldn't have arranged such perfect symmetry.

As they got to the point where the trail curved from the creek to come toward the bridge, I prepared to stand up to let them pass in a minute. But instead of continuing to stick to the trail, they kept going along the creek, at a steady height, going through the thick underbrush, ignoring the ground's dip down to the branch and back up, and again, the trees.

I let my breath out, so relieved they weren't coming my way, after all. I couldn't believe how glad I was to be still alive. But I wasn't about to investigate any further by following them, whatever the hell they were.

Dream Messages

Maura O'Connell

In 2002 and 2003, I experienced two separate dreams where two of my friends died. Within three months after each dream, the friend who had appeared in that dream collapsed and had to be rushed to the emergency room, both times with lung infections. Two dreams, two friends, two lung infections. I am certain about the timing because I was keeping a dream journal at that time.

During that same two-year period, I had a third dream. In this one, my sister died. I woke up the morning after this dream and called her; she was alive and well. I asked her how she was doing, and she said she was fine. We chatted a bit more, and then I asked, "So, are you really doing okay?"

"Um, well...no," she finally admitted. "Why do you ask?"

"Because I had a dream about you." That was all I said; I didn't tell her any specifics.

"I've kind of got this lung thing going on," she said. Apparently, she was feeling some pain in one of her lungs. My sister has always been reluctant to go to conventional doctors, or take any conventional medicine like antibiotics. So, I gave her all the details about the other two dreams and said, "You really, *really* need to see a doctor for this."

She did, and she got the medications she needed, and she was fine.

In the Shadow of Cinder Butte

Nate Barse

Let me tell you about the time I was shot. I was 16 years old and it was high summer in the sprawling metropolis of Eden, Idaho, population 365. My father and I were living in an old office trailer which had been converted into a "luxury two-bedroom trailer home," as we used to say. It was tucked in between one of the town's two bars and one of the town's two gas stations. It wasn't much to look at, but it had a nice yard and a little shed for all of dad's tools and projects. We were pretty comfortable there.

It was around 8 o'clock in the evening and the sun was just starting to kiss the horizon. My dad was next door at the Trophy Club playing in his regular Wednesday night dart league and helping out behind the bar. I was just hanging out in the kitchen watching TV.

At some point, my attention was diverted from the TV by what I thought was a sort of high pitched whistling noise just on the edge of hearing. I cocked my head to the side a little to try to determine the source and direction of the sound when two things seemed to happen simultaneously: I felt a sharp sting on the back of my neck and strong WHACK in the middle of my back that knocked me out of the chair and onto the floor.

I sat dazed for a moment trying to figure out what had just happened. I reached up to my neck to investigate the pain there and my fingers came away dotted with flecks of blood. "What the hell?" I said. I looked at the chair in confusion. Then I looked at the window behind the chair thinking maybe a wasp or hornet or something got in somehow and stung me, but the window was closed.

That was when I noticed the hole in the wall a few inches below the window sill. The faux-wood paneling was splintered out around a hole about the size of a dime. I looked at the smooth unbroken surface of the front face of the chair back. Then back at the hole in the wall.

Next I turned the chair around and saw a matching hole in the faux-wicker covering of the back of the chair. My eyes traveled back and forth between the hole in the wall and the hole in the chair, still trying to puzzle out what was going on. When I turned the chair back around to look at the front again, I heard a slight rattling from inside the hollow back of the chair. Something clicked in my brain.

"Holy shit," I shouted, "I think I just got shot!"

Adrenaline kicked in and I started freaking out. I looked around frantically trying to find cover in my living room in case more bullets came flying in when my eyes locked on the stainless steel mini-freezer. I scrambled across the kitchen floor and hunkered down behind the freezer.

I thought, "Bullets aren't gonna get through this thing!" I cowered there for several minutes expecting the Wild West show to continue in my living room.

No more bullets arrived. After the adrenaline surge subsided and my reason returned, I decided it was ok to come out from behind the freezer.

Not entirely convinced of the safety of the situation, I crawled across the kitchen again to the telephone. I called my dad at the Trophy Club and told him to come quick because I just got shot at. I had to repeat myself a couple times to be heard over the bar noise in the background. I think it was more the urgency in the tone of my voice than the content of my words that convinced him.

He came home a couple minutes later and we looked at the holes together. I thought he was skeptical at first, but the holes and the rattling inside the chair seemed to convince him.

We called 911 and they sent out a Jerome County sheriff's deputy. The deputy took my statement in a polite but slightly disinterested manner.

It wasn't until he and my dad took the chair apart that he started to take me seriously. He held the slug up between his thumb and forefinger and said, "I reckon that's a .306 rifle slug. Probably came from a long ways off. Maybe the other side of Cinder Butte. Couldn't 've been no closer. Otherwise the bullet would've gone clean through you and out the other side of the trailer. You're lucky the trajectory wasn't three inches higher. Then that bullet would've come in through the window, over the top of the chair, and hit you right in the spine between your shoulder blades. Could've kill't ya or crippled ya."

I wanted to keep the bullet and put it on a chain to wear around my neck like Huck Finn, but the deputy said he had to keep it for evidence.

Looking at the guts of the chair and seeing the ¼-inch of stuffing that was the only thing between my flesh and the Hereafter sent a chill right through my soul. I can't rightly say if it was the Hand of God, my own latent telekinetic powers, or the pure entropic forces of a vast and mysterious Universe that stopped that bullet. At this point, I don't think it matters much. I'm alive to tell the tale and grateful for it.

The Storm

Martin Kleinman

What I remember most about the storm was how the young woman who would later become my wife cried and cried her blue eyes out even after the sun rose, clean and clear, the following morning.

This happened in a New York City long ago and far away. In those days, the seventies, whole precincts stood dangerous, derelict. Entire Manhattan buildings could be purchased for the price of a nicely equipped Mercedes Benz.

Such buildings existed in the West Village. Beyond the blood puddles of the Meatpacking District were row upon row of refrigerated warehouses and, close by, the eighteen wheelers that delivered dead animals to the wholesale food purveyors that serviced a hungry city.

By dusk, those semis stood silent, their trailers unlocked.

But late at night, during those post-Stonewall, pre-AIDS days, those truck trailers became a gathering place for legions of gays, who hopped inside, inhaled amyl nitrite, and engaged in anonymous sex.

It was an area called, simply, "The Trucks."

Back then, a lifetime ago, I fell head over heels in love with a young woman who travelled in a circle of friends far different from the folks I grew up with. I was from Sparta. She was from Athens. That is, I was an outer borough, white ethnic provincial and she was from the affluent suburbs and involved in the theater world. Many of her friends were gay and some of them went to The Trucks.

And, in retrospect, many of them were not enamored of the fact that their darling straight woman friend began a relationship with the likes of me. "Are you still seeing Bronxy," they'd tease.

This woman of mine lived on Morton Street in the West Village. As our relationship progressed, I spent more and more time in this unfamiliar land and far less time in my place in a Hopperesque, careworn quadrant of the city.

In time, our union evolved to the point where we, as some at the time said, "never came up for air." We stayed indoors all weekend, in that second floor apartment of hers, under the covers, stopping only to order food, never answering the phone.

Some of her friends understood. Others, especially her two dearest, gay, theater friends, did not. And one of these was far less understanding, and far more vocal, than the other.

Which brings me to the storm. That Saturday night, she buzzed me in and, even from the hallway, I could hear her crying. She later told me that her two besties had, unsuccessfully, tried to convince her to ditch me and come out partying with them, never mind the rain. Their plan was to drive in from

Long Island, after a day of family visits, and then hit the clubs. They tried to convince her that she was ruining her life, hitching her wagon to the wrong star. That is, me.

I was emerging as her future. Yet I was still the newcomer to her world.

My girlfriend was conflicted. I was not. I wanted, expected—hell, craved—her full attention. She loved me, and I her. Yet she cherished her dear friends in a way that the immature me did not fully comprehend. Over the years, she and her buddies had shared many college theater company adventures, late nights at the Paradise Garage, cuddly sleepovers, pints of Haagen Dazs, and double-features at the Theater 80.

"What are you doing with *him*?" her best friend railed. I'll call him "T."

"Come dancing with us! What's wrong with you?" T pushed.

"Oh, I'm going to hang up," T screamed, frustrated. "You're giving me a colossal headache."

"So lay off the poppers already," she told him.

"Oh that's it, Blanche!" T screamed. "That is *it*! What, are you in love or something?"

Her silence told him the story. He clicked.

The winds picked up as the evening progressed. We stayed in and, as was our wont, remained under the covers in the bedroom of her Morton Street apartment. Around eleven, the rain began to come down in sheets. It scoured the sidewalks and rattled the fire escape on the front-facing windows. From time to time, we'd hear the footsteps of people running down the street, fumbling with their keys, trying desperately to get inside, and out of the rain.

Normally, summer storms in New York City end rather quickly. Not this one. It seemed to pick up steam with each passing minute, until the wind howled like the twister that transported Dorothy to Oz. The rain pelted the windows with such force that I thought for sure it would bash them in and soak the entire apartment.

"I'm getting scared," she said, pulling the covers tighter around her neck.

"Relax, it's just a passing storm," I said, using the occasion to cuddle still closer.

Boom! At that moment, something or someone crashed into the fire escape window. She screamed, ducked under the covers and yelled, "Do something!"

I bolted upright and, powered by a rush of adrenalin, threw off the covers and jiggled over to the window. On the way, I notice the time on the Sony's cable box: eleven fifty.

Boom! A bolt of lightning bisected the West Village sky and in that flash of white light, I saw, or thought I saw, a large, dark figure on the fire escape.

It knocked on the window.

It groaned miserably.

"What is it? What is it?" She began to panic.

I ran into the kitchen and got a chef's knife from the wooden block on the counter.

"WHAT IS IT?" she screamed.

The figure moaned and banged on the window again and, reflexively, I jumped back and tried to focus. The creature, whatever it was, rammed its black head onto the glass.

I stepped forward. Another bolt of lightning pierced the night and afforded a good look.

It was a huge black cat. Actually, this was more of a panther then a cat. It was a snarling, seething beast that seemed to take up the entire fire escape.

"It's a cat!" I told her. "The fucking biggest black cat in the world."

74

"Well, make it go away," she said, more crying than screaming at this point. "Just make...it...go... away!!!!"

I had never seen her more out of control, more hysterical than at that very moment. And, I felt glad. I admit it. I was glad, not because she was *scared*, but because she wanted me to protect her from harm, from demons real and imagined, and that she needed me, really needed *me*, in a visceral, Tarzan-like way.

The clock on the cable box said twelve-oh-two.

I strode to the window and banged on the window with the handle of the knife, but the beast would not startle, nor be scared off.

Instead, it twisted its body, as if in agony, and pawed at the window frantically, desperately, refusing to either jump to the street below, or move up the fire escape. I feared for the cat, feared that it would break the glass and cut its fool head open.

The rain pelted down, harder still. I went back to the bed, and slid under the covers.

"Let's just go to sleep," I said.

"I can't."

"Try," I said. "Because it's not leaving. And I'm not opening up the window to let it in." Boom! Thunder exploded and, simultaneously, lightning again lit up the street.

And then the streetlights went out, just like that.

She sat bolt upright in the bed, shivering uncontrollably. I hummed the theme to the folksy television show, *The Waltons*. Whenever she awoke from a bad dream, this usually did the trick. I held her close and kissed the top of her head as I hummed.

Lightning sliced the sky again. We held our breath for the next explosion of thunder.

And then the telephone rang.

"Don't pick it up," she said.

"OK."

It kept ringing.

"Make it stop," she said.

I picked up the receiver of her bedside phone and then slammed it down. I went back under the covers and continued to hum.

The phone rang again.

It wouldn't stop.

"Something's wrong," I said, throwing off the covers. I picked up the phone.

At that moment, the banging of the beast at the window suddenly ceased. Our black cat was finally gone. "Thank God!" I thought.

It was an Officer Riordan, of the Nassau County Highway Patrol Bureau.

"What's the matter, officer?" I asked. "Is there a problem?"

And here, dear reader, I truly want you to believe that every word I say is true.

Riordan begins to answer. He affects that flat, all-business law enforcement tone used when they try to keep things calm.

"Who is it?" she asks, as I nod and talk to Riordan. She fairly jumps out of the bed. "Give me the phone," she says.

She grabs it out of my hand and, as she talks, her face morphs from annoyed, to confused, to crumpled in pain, before my very eyes.

Riordan is at North Shore Hospital on Long Island. He is with T's mother, who sobs and screams bloody murder in the background.

Riordan explains. T and some friends drive back into the city, in the rain. They laugh. They anticipate a night of wild fun. T is behind the wheel. T, suddenly, holds both hands to his head and shrieks in agony. A thunderclap of pain. T barely manages to pull onto the shoulder of the Turnpike. Says he can't see straight. He vomits all over himself. T's friend in the front seat slides behind the wheel, drives to the hospital, right up to the ER entry. A gurney, a team of doctors. Tests, lights, tubes.

Aneurysm.

Like a flash of lightning, T is gone.

Forty years ago, and I remember every detail of that stormy night. She drops the phone, clutches me, convulses in sobs.

Riordan concludes. The time of death, my hand to God, was eleven fifty.

The Monkey Gangs

Robert P. Kaye

In the 1980s, I visited Jaipur, India, with my first wife, flying in from Delhi while my suitcase went off to Bangladesh. We toured the Pink City in the desert: camels in the street, men in turbans and women in embroidered mirrorwork skirts. The picturesque heat, dust and the relics of Maharajas that comprised the foundation of the tourist economy.

We visited the Jantar Mantar, a collection of fixed astronomical instruments on the scale of buildings two and a half centuries ago. We wandered among the structures made of marble and pink sandstone, some four stories tall, like the scattered blocks of a giant child. One looked like an epic skate park ramp, another a concave bowl with sections cut out like random slices from a melon rind. One resembled a three-dimensional Georgia O'Keefe painting—a vulva. The sundial kept time to two-second accuracy, the sun's edge advancing the breath of a hand each minute. I knew nothing about astronomy and could only wonder at the distant science behind the shapes. No explicit memory of interaction with my wife remains, which probably means we didn't argue.

After the observatory, we went to a group of shops across a busy road for refreshment. Dense trees provided shelter from the sun. The tables and chairs were occupied and some sort of performance in progress. A tribe of rhesus macaques screeched above, each about the size of a two-year-old. Monkey gangs roamed the city with impunity so nobody seemed to take notice. We stood focusing on the entertainment while drinking hypersugared sodas and *nimbu pani*, the lime version of lemonade.

A screaming tornado erupted overhead, monkeys tearing around as if trying to rip the trees out of the ground, a canopy full of horror movie sound effects. A monkey dropped off a branch directly onto my head and shoulder, causing me to stagger, the man beside me knocked flat on his face.

The monkey had voided its bowels as it came down out of the tree, spattering my shirt and pants with shit. The fallen man's wife helped him up from the flagstones, his nose apparently broken, glasses askew, camera lens shattered, acrid monkey diarrhea mixing with his blood.

The crowd looked at the stunned man—fiftyish, broad nosed, probably from Goa—and some of them laughed. His wife began to scream at the crowd in English. "You monsters, we come to your city and my husband is injured and you think this is funny?" She hurled recriminations as her husband stood unsteady, eyes unfocused, blood from his nose flowing onto a shirtfront of monkey shit.

I don't know if the monkeys remained in the tree watching or not. We left with the woman still shouting, me attempting to daub fecal matter off my shirt and pants with a handful of damp napkins, only managing to spread it around.

That night we had dinner with an older couple, friends of friends, in a hotel restaurant looking down on Jaipur. I wore a newly purchased *kurta paijama*, its own brand of white guy discomfort. The husband proclaimed the superiority of arranged marriages, how they always worked out for the best, while his wife told my first wife that such was not the case, that love matches were far superior.

This is what I remember. Not the nature of the performance in the restaurant courtyard or whether my first wife and I were getting along at that moment. Not what we had for dinner or where we went next on the trip. I remember the tornado of conflict, the impact on my head and right shoulder, the acrid smell of shit and screamed accusations. The equal dysfunction of arranged and love marriages. Alien instruments on a large scale, designed to divine astronomical principles I still fail to understand. The casual banditry of monkey gangs.

The Dead Hours

Wanda Morrow Clevenger

I realized with each step across the yellow cypress flooring and turn at the walk-in closet (where I pushed shut the door that seemed to always be ajar) and into the bath, that the twisting threads of lavender smoke growing thick inside my nostrils were only exacerbating my fear. "Leave this house," I said again and again, the bravado spoken just loud enough to surpass my thrumming heartbeat. Burning sage in these situations cleanses the space I was told, but I only had the thin lavender sticks left over from a Christmas gift, stored away when Monte claimed they stunk up the house—like his cigarettes were a breath of fresh air.

The swarm of goosebumps standing at high alert on the back of my neck raced down my arms then and I gripped the incense stone tighter and looked directly to the empty outlet on the north bathroom wall where the pink, ribbed shell nightlight had repeatedly flipped on. Not that I expected it might still hug the outlet, I had after all tugged it free of the wall when four times logic was defied, and banished this entity to the burn barrel. Come morning, though, should the agitator reappear on my porch, a stronger fix than sage or lavender or Monte's cigarettes was indicated. I didn't allow focus on anything else, most especially the mirrors or shower curtain, and said again, "Leave this house."

When Eileen came near, in the same dead hours the experts claim these others rise, and rolled up and over the end of the bed and over the length of me, stirring a chilled breeze in her wake, I yelped and fumbled for the bedside lamp. Eileen fled the light, fled the gory site of her suicide as quickly as she had come. She was my first visitor and I told no one.

The night I woke pre-dawn and couldn't fall back into sleep—the room so black and pressing—I concentrated on the droning electric fan blades, the same propeller sound imagined in Al Stewart's song "Flying Sorcery," while waiting for a dream to feather me away to Al's safe, melodious year of the cat. In this inert span a rush of air surged through the fan blades, a rev of iced breath followed by an immediate bouncing weight. I lay under this frightening weight some confused seconds until forcing an ingrained plea, "Leave me, in the name of the Father and the Son and the Holy Spirit." The bouncing stopped; the fan blades slowed to normal.

I named the dining room's southwest ceiling thump after the boy who dangled nude from a barn rafter. The freckled redhead often stayed overnight, crashing with my son in the bunk bed placed upstairs in that otherwise quiet corner. The bunk bed was outgrown and given away in time, but the frequent thump that duplicates the hard landing of someone from the top bunk to the floor, remains.

When the shampoo cap jumped upwards of its empty bottle and clipped the back of my right leg, I scooped up the purple plastic cup and sailed it over the shower curtain rod, saying as authoritatively as I could muster in my soapy birthday suit, "Enough of this bull."

Keeping silent about these events has gained me no solid ground, I look or feel the fool either way. Some spirits attach themselves to places and people, maybe in effort to explain wrongful action. I can't claim to understand, only know speculation flies in the face of faith. Of the pranks played, no physical harm has been done as yet and sleep aids line the pharmacy shelves. Radios drown out aberrant noises. Houses settle and creak in the night.

Eileen's house was bulldozed years back, but not before later renters heard her washing dishes in the kitchen sink in the dead hours. And of all the unsettled energy lingering near and about, I find Eileen's presence most intriguing—this soul who took care to wrap a plastic bag around her head before popping a bullet into her brain. If I was inclined to mock those who die by their own hand (and I never shall) I'd say for someone so utterly determined to leave this world, she doesn't appear in much of a hurry to go.

February 1977

Christine Conte

I'm eight years old and it's school vacation week. I'm with my parents in San Juan, Puerto Rico. Staying at a Holiday Inn right on the Atlantic Ocean beach. We check in during the late afternoon.

I'm full on, at 100% power. First time on an airplane, first time this far from home.

The hotel has a casino, and my parents are excited about that.

And I'm super-excited about swimming. That's all I want to do. It's February and I haven't gone swimming since late summer/early fall. From school's-out to back-to-school, you can't get me out of the pool. You'll have to pry my blue shriveled fingers off the ladder to get me out. "You spend too much time underwater," my mother always complains, and I'll dive down, do a handstand on the bottom of the pool, and wiggle my feet at her.

I've been staring at pictures of the impossibly bluegreen Atlantic Ocean in the glossy brochures my parents got from the travel agent. I've been daydreaming and nightdreaming about it for weeks.

The largest body of water I've ever been in is the Long Island Sound. The protected Connecticut coast gets such gentle, rolling waves, swells rolling back and forth between Connecticut and the north shore of Long Island, a continuous game of catch. My parents tell a story of friends who moved to Connecticut from Wisconsin. The first time they saw the Sound, they asked, "What lake is that?" It's like a lake, really.

My mother says I'm a good swimmer.

She herself doesn't really like to swim. She'll go in the pool to cool off, but she freaks out if she gets wet above the neck. She'll just cling to a floaty toy, raise her chin, scrunch up her nose, close her eyes, and purse her lips tight. A more extreme version of the face you make when a dog is licking your face and you don't want their tongue to accidentally go in your mouth. She often jokes, or *maybe* jokes, that she made my dad buy our house because it was high on a hill and she could never drown there. We can see the Long Island Sound from our front lawn during the winter when the trees are bare.

The palm trees around the hotel sway in the warm breeze like a cliché. Just a few hours ago, we were lugging our suitcases through snow and slush to JFK.

And tomorrow I would swim in the bluegreen ocean!

It's a long night spent holed up in the hotel room. We leave only to go out to eat at a steakhouse nearby. For dessert, I have something called *flan*. It's the most memorable food item of the trip. I have it again a few more times before we leave.

Back at the hotel, it's getting dark and we have the window open. We can hear people whistling outside. It's strange, but I like it. Later, my parents send me down the hall with an ice bucket and money for sodas and snacks. There's a balcony railing along the open hallway. I stop at the balcony and listen to the people whistling. I can't see who's out there in the dark. A few people are walking around, dressed up so beautifully and laughing, going back to their rooms from the casino. But it's not them whistling. I whistle back, in the same two-note, low-high call. They go silent for a little while, and then start again. They whistle all night long. My parents grumble about it. I find it so soothing.

In the morning, we finally head over to the beach. A short walk past the pool and through an open gate. Sand and ocean and sky for miles. The smell of salt and cocoa butter. A leather-skinned beachcomber sits outside the gate selling driftwood sculptures to tourists. People laughing and shouting in Spanish and English. Brown glistening bodies.

The ocean is even bluegreener than mere photos in a travel brochure could ever convey.
We find a space to lay down our towels and we set up camp. My mother leaves not an inch of freckled Irish skin unprotected from the tropical UV rays. Hat and

sunglasses and a steamy romance novel. My dad and I, however, came for sun and sea, and we shall have all the sun and sea.

We leave her ashore and head for the water's edge. The sand is hot and clean. I do the ow-ow-ow walk all the way there. I finally stand on the cooler wet sand. Fluffy white clouds contrast against the ridiculously blue sky. The bluegreen waves rise offshore and zoom in so bluegreenly, falling and ending in a backwash of foam and pebbles and seaweed wrapped around my delighted ankles.

I'm about the happiest I've ever been.

We swim and play in the water for a long time.

The strength of the waves takes me a little while to get used to, but I don't go out too far. I recognize the hugeness of it all. I feel...respect and reverence, I guess...but no fear.

My dad after a while goes back on land to get some rays. I stay in the water, because bluegreen.

I have my goggles and swim underwater sometimes. The water is so clean and clear, I can find seashells at the bottom and see fishes sometimes. I look out to the beach and locate my parents every once in a while. They're next to the people with the red and white beach umbrella.

After a long time, I suddenly realize I'm a lot farther out in the bluegreen than I ever planned to be. And now I'm way over, diagonal to where my parents are. I can just about see the red and white beach umbrella waaayyyy over there. People on the beach are very small. There's nobody else near me.

And—whoa!—I can't feel the bottom any more.

While I'm thinking about this and treading water, a wave swells up behind me and pulls me straight down in a strong tumultuous rush. The taste of salt water in my nostrils, frantically paddling and kicking to get back up to the surface.

And boom, I sink and I'm at the bottom.

Lying there at the bottom, in maybe 15 feet of clear water, I can feel sand and seashells and rocks under me. Shells are pointy and rough against my skin. The rocks are smooth lumps. The sand is soft as velvet.

I'm looking straight up from the ocean floor and can see the sun and sky way up there. Sunlight sparkling on the surface, rolling and dancing and rippling.

It's so quiet and calm and pretty here.

I don't know how long I'm here, enchanted by how lovely it all is.

It feels like a really long time.

The surface of the water above me is a soft and rippling panoramic movie screen.

I watch the ripply fluffy white clouds sail across the ridiculously blue ripply sky.

Sunlight bends and bounces and bobs and plays on the water.

Enchanting. Unreal, but as real as can be.

I think about the people who whistle outside in the dark all night.

Who are they and why do they whistle outside in the dark all night?

I liked them for some reason. I liked their whistling. It's soothing.

Mommy and Daddy are up there on their beach towels, next to the people with the red and white beach umbrella.

I wonder if I'll see them again. Or my sister or Max our dog or my teacher Mrs. Tanezzio.

I just don't know.

Still, I'm the happiest I've ever been.

Everything is safe and peaceful and lovely.

I'm okay with this all.

Then—WHOOSH—

I feel something or someone yank me back up to the surface in the same kind of turbulent rush that pulled me down.

Speeding up through the water like the penguins in Antarctica that we saw in a film at school. The penguins zoom up from under the water and jump up onto the ice like little bird bullets.

At the top, I cough and I cough and I cough for a long time, feverishly treading water.

Heart racing, I can finally breathe again.

There's nobody around.

I swim for the shore as fast as I can, choking back tears.

I cough and cough some more once in the shallows. Kneeling in the wet sand at the water's edge.

I make my way down the hot sand to find my parents, dodging blankets and coolers and brown glistening bodies. That red and white beach umbrella is a beacon, a lighthouse to guide me home.

Finally I flop down on my mother's towel and throw my arms around her.

"I almost drowned!" I cry.

"Oh, you did not," my mother says, barely looking away from the steamy romance novel. "You're fine. Now get off me, it's too hot."

I try to explain, but they shut me down.

I never talk about it ever again to anyone, but I know it happened.

And I learn later that those weren't people whistling outside in the dark all night.

They're tiny little tree frogs called *coquis*.

When they whistle, they're talking to each other.

Calling out to their families and friends, I guess, to make sure everybody's okay.

They stay up in the palm trees where they won't drown, like my mother living in a house high on a hill.

For the rest of the trip, I like to think they're calling out to make sure I'm okay.

I know *they* would believe me, even if nobody else does.

The bluegreen *did* try to keep me that day.

It just changed its mind.

I still don't know why.

The Truth about Pheromones

Martha Grover

Three weeks ago, I had sex with a guy I met on OkCupid. We met at a Chinese restaurant on Hawthorne. He said hi and introduced himself and then he told me I looked nice. This was my fifth date with someone I'd met on OkCupid, and this was the first time that any of my dates had complimented me about anything, least of all, on my appearance. It felt nice. I was surprised actually, by how nice it felt.

On our second date we got drunk at a bar. He told me "You're so smart it's kind of intimidating." Apparently the evidence for this was that I've watched a lot of nature documentaries and had told him fun facts about fratricide and pseudo-penises among female spotted-hyenas in Africa. Anyway, I changed the subject after he said this. It made me a little suspicious actually; men that are intimidated by a woman's intelligence scare me. There is a difference between being scared and being intimidated. Besides, I didn't believe his statement anyway.

We made out in his car and then in my car. It felt good to kiss someone. I knew I would have hickies and bruises on my breasts later but it seemed worth it at the time.

He asked me if I wanted to come home with him. I can't, I said. I don't have my medication with me.

What medicine? he said.

If I don't take it, it'll ruin my day tomorrow, I said.

Well come over on Sunday, he said. And bring your medicine.

I didn't tell him that not taking my medication would actually ruin two days total. And that if I didn't take it for three days my body would start to shut down. And that there is a big difference between medicine and medication.

Okay, we'll hang out on Sunday, I said.

That Sunday, as I merged onto I-84 West, I turned on the radio to a program about cranes. They were interviewing a biologist who'd worked his whole life trying to protect endangered cranes. He described the lives of cranes, where they lived, how one of their biggest populations lives in the DMZ between North and South Korea, how cranes have been an important part of Japanese and other cultural traditions.

The interviewer asked the biologist why cranes were so loved by us humans. Cranes look like humans, he replied. They have long legs like us, they live as long as us (at least in captivity), they dance like us. In fact, he said, cranes are one of the few animals that truly dance like humans. They have these ornate and complicated mating dances that they do.

I wondered what the cranes are thinking when they do their mating dance. Are they worried they won't remember the steps? That they'll fuck it up? Do they worry that when they're dancing, they're not expressing their own individuality? Or are they in lock-step like soldiers doing drills? One time on the radio, I heard a woman from the Freedom Singers say that if it were not for music, the civil rights movement might never have happened. The music, the ritual, the lyrics and the rhythm of it, the rigid form of the songs, gave the protestors courage.

We had sushi. I finished a bottle of wine at his apartment. He sat down on the couch next to me and started kissing my face, my neck. He took off my shirt and started kissing my breasts. We went down the hallway into his dark bedroom. He asked me if I wanted the lights on or off, which seemed irrelevant to me. I told him to keep them off.

He wanted me to be on top, not surprising, considering he was overweight and from what I'd gathered before, led a rather sedentary life. The only problem is that I've never been very good at being on top especially when I don't know someone very well. I don't know why, it's something about my rhythm. Something's always just a little off. I got on top anyway. But after a bit, it just didn't feel right. It wasn't fun. I rolled off him.

"What's wrong?" he said.

I sighed. "I don't know, this is the first sex I've had in a year," I said. "I guess I'm just trying to wrap my head around it. That's all." This was partly true. What was I doing here anyway? All of a sudden the scenario seemed wrong. Not what I'd pictured.

He didn't say anything. Both of us just lay there for a few minutes.

"I'm sorry," I said.

"That's okay." A few more minutes of silence. Finally he got up and walked out of the room. I heard the toilet flush and he came back and got in bed.

I do want to have sex though, I said to myself.

"Here," I said. "Get on top of me."

"What?"

"Just lay on top of me."

"Are you sure?"

I nodded. He got on top of me but I could tell he was still tense, propping himself up slightly on his elbows.

"No, you need to relax," I said.

"I'm going to crush you."

"No, you're not. Don't worry, just relax." I breathed in and out fully, to show him that he wasn't going to crush me, as men often think they are going to do. I wanted to show him that I was going to be fine.

After a few seconds, I felt his body relaxing on top of me. I've always felt this position to be very relaxing. That is, lying under a large man. It reminds me of the animal behaviorist, Temple Grandin's, book *Animals in Translation* where she talks about how being autistic, for her, is like being a cow; she built herself a compression box when she was a teenager. It was a box that would press down on her sides when she climbed inside it; if she was feeling anxious, it calmed her down. This is the same effect being in tightly-packed herds has on cows. Farmers put cows in compression devices before they give them their immunization shots so they won't get too anxious.

"Here, get inside of me," I said. And we had sex.

He came, but I didn't. I asked him to finish me off with his hands. He put his hand on my clitoris. He started rubbing, and then paused. "Do you like up and down or round and round?" he asked.

This question annoyed me, like he was asking me how I wanted my steak cooked. "I don't care," I said.

After I came, we talked a little bit in his too-soft bed. I told him I couldn't have children. "The only reason I even have a period," I said, "is because I take birth control. I take it just for the estrogen. And even then I still don't have a period sometimes."

"You're like a unicorn," he said.

"What do you mean?"

"A woman who doesn't have her period, a unicorn."

I still didn't really understand what he meant by this, although I knew, whatever he meant, that it was insensitive. I didn't say anything.

"You don't want to have kids," I said.

"No. There's enough people on this planet." He sighed and looked up at the ceiling.

"Yeah, it's insane," I said, becoming a little animated. "It's terrifying to think about how many people are living. I recently visited a website that calculates all the births and deaths on earth every ten seconds. It was horrifying." I rolled over so I was facing him and put one arm over his body.

"Yeah, what we need is another black plague," he whispered into my face.

"That's really sexy," I said.

We both started giggling. Our bellies touched, and I could feel his stomach jump up and down. We both laughed for what seemed like a long time.

I asked him if he wanted to go to the Sandy River with me the next day. He said yes. This plan is going to work perfectly for me, I thought. I had dinner plans that night in Portland anyway. I could go to the river and then drop him off at his apartment on the way back into town. Theoretically I was supposed to be working from home, but I could always do that work later. I had my whole day planned out. I said goodnight.

He fell asleep fast and started snoring, loud. Eventually, I moved into the living room and tried to sleep on his couch. But I could hear his snoring even from the couch and so only intermittently slept all through the night.

In the morning we went to breakfast, and I asked him if there was anything he wanted to know about me. He asked me what I thought about the new batch of superhero movies that had recently been produced. I didn't quite believe he'd actually just asked me this and so we talked about the new batch of superhero movies until I said that they usually make these kinds of movies for a global audience and that they had to give the back stories of the superheroes so that people in China would understand what was going on. Then he looked as if I had just told him that Santa Claus wasn't real and so I changed the subject.

The sky was still overcast when we left the breakfast place. "Maybe we shouldn't go to the river," I said, looking doubtfully at the sky.

"Yeah, besides we both stayed up late. Maybe it would be better to just relax today."

I just nodded even though going to the river did seem like relaxing to me. The only problem was that, now that I wasn't going to the river, I didn't want to go home to Gresham and work from home, only to have to drive back into Portland that night. I also didn't want to go to a coffee shop because I find them uncomfortable to hang out in for more than an hour. "Well, then do you mind if I hang out at your house today and get some work done?" I asked.

He said that would be fine, however when I got back to his house, I was so tired from lack of sleep that I fell asleep on his couch while he went out to run some errands. My phone rang in the middle of the nap. I stumbled into his bedroom where my phone was charging on the floor. It was my friend Michael. "Did I wake you up?"

"Uh...."

"It sounds like I woke you up."

I admitted that he had woken me up. He asked what I'd been up to. I wanted to tell him that I'd had sex for the first time in a year the night before with a man that I wasn't even attracted to. But I didn't say this because I was sitting on his bed at the time and it just seemed wrong, and mean. And then I felt trapped in his apartment. Like it was some kind of prison, like I was on this train that was moving in one direction and I was just along for the ride. "I'll tell you about it later," I said.

I could have gathered my things and left, but instead, I got off the phone and went back to sleep on the couch.

He woke me up later and we had a Caesar salad together and watched a nature documentary about humpback whales and then had sex again, this time on his couch.

After we both got dressed, I sat back down on the couch and started doing computer work for my boss at the coffee-table.

He got on his computer and started looking at photo-shopped pictures of cats on Reddit, periodically tugging at his penis through his pajama pants. And this was when I started to feel weird about seeing him again in the future, not just the fact that I was here now, in his apartment, instead of at home or at a coffee shop. It was becoming clear to me that this guy wasn't anyone I really ever wanted to see again. There were several things that weren't right to me and I started to tick them off in my head: First of all, his question about the superhero movies when he could have asked me something about me. The fact that he hadn't done any artwork since he graduated from design school two years ago and seemed uninterested in creating anything ever again. The fact that he seemed uninterested in the drawings of mine that I'd shown him. Although he was overweight, he was apparently totally unmotivated to lose weight, a fact he'd bluntly told me the night before. His apartment smelled like cologne. Like he'd spilled an entire bottle of cologne into the dirty carpet. The bathroom smelled like cigarettes and when I asked him why, he said it was something with the pipes and that it was his neighbors. I felt like he was lying. He'd said that he doesn't think hairy underarms on women are sexy, and that he knows this doesn't make him sound like a feminist. He kept using words incorrectly like, conductive instead of conducive. And lastly, I just wasn't that attracted to him.

Nevertheless, despite all of this, I still had sex with him one more time before I left that day.

Afterward, after I had gotten home and taken a shower, after I'd emailed him and told him that I wasn't going to be hanging out with him again, I couldn't figure out why I had had sex with him to begin with. Perhaps the first time made sense. But then, why didn't I just leave? Was having sex two more times with a guy I wasn't that into better than a commute to Gresham and back? Better than sitting in a coffee shop all day instead of his stinky apartment? This couldn't possibly be my decision-making process. I didn't have a good answer. And to not have an answer wasn't acceptable. I was an adult after all, I should have an answer as to why I do, or don't have sex with someone.

In medicine, when they can't come up with a cause for a disease, they call it idiopathic. I've always thought the word sounded like idiot. The idiot's path. I'd had idiopathic sex. Had I been infected with a mind-control parasite, like those ones that make ants walk up stalks of grass so they can get eaten by prey and then pooped out to begin the parasite's life cycle all over again?

All through the next week, I thought about it and thought about it. Maybe I was like those cranes. Somehow I'd become locked into this mating dance with this guy and it had become impossible to extricate myself. Maybe it had to do with hormones. Five years ago I found out I had idiopathic Cushing's disease. And for a bunch of reasons that don't really matter enough to explain, I'm now taking every hormone a person can take except for testosterone. My endocrinologist told me that I'd probably had low estrogen since puberty. I'd only started taking estrogen pills a little before I'd broken up with my ex-boyfriend. Maybe it was this estrogen that made me have sex with this guy.

Driving into Portland for a teacher training, I thought about it, how it used to take me forever to orgasm and how when I did, it was okay. Now that I take estrogen, my orgasms are much, much better. I remembered how a couple months ago I'd told my sister Sarah this. "I think it's the estrogen," I'd said.

"Well you're in your thirties," she said. "You're at your sexual peak." Sarah is a nurse and is regarded in our family as being a medical authority.

"Yeah, but does that account for the quality of orgasm?" I asked her.

She said yes.

I doubted her. Something about this explanation didn't seem right. And if it was right, did this also mean that I was due for lots more sex with men I wasn't really attracted to?

I ran into a friend at the training and she chatted with me outside while I smoked a cigarette in the parking lot. Of course I told her about my experience with the guy from OkCupid.

"Ugh, I don't know why I had sex with that guy," I muttered.

"Well, why did you?"

"I guess I felt kind of pressured into it," I said, and the moment I said it I knew it wasn't true. In no way was I pressured into it. But it was easier to say this than to say I didn't know, again.

I went home and did some research about the rise in women's libido in their thirties. First of all, the rise of libido in women in their thirties is entirely self-reported. Furthermore, all libido really means is sex drive, not the actual pleasure derived from sex. The studies also imply sex with another person. Not masturbation. There are so many factors, like confidence, self-esteem, and emotional maturity that play a part here, that I wasn't convinced that my estrogen level had anything to do with libido. My libido has remained constant over the last fifteen years or so. Besides, most women have constant estrogen levels until menopause. I didn't fit within this construct.

I thought back on the last ten years of my sex life. Before I was diagnosed with Cushing's, in my early and mid-twenties, sex, to me, had been either an entirely emotional affair, or else athletic—akin to asking someone to play a rigorous game of badminton with me. I never felt that some invisible tractor beam was pulling me toward someone. I'd always been in control. It was always a decision I had made, a line in the sand. However, this recent sex had been something different; I didn't feel in control at all. It had just happened. I somehow had lost all my personal agency and I wasn't sure why. Could the estrogen have made me act this way?

And then I remembered pheromones. But, I thought, I've never really believed in pheromones—those invisible chemicals known to mysteriously influence human sexuality. They always seemed like mumbo jumbo to me. It's not as if I don't believe in science. Science saves my life every day in the form of little white pills synthesized from porcine hormones. It's just that the existence of pheromones has never jived with my own lived experience. In all my sexual encounters, I had never felt the invisible pull of someone's body. Everything has always been very visible.

A week later, at a family baby shower, I talked with my cousin Donald and told him I didn't know why I had had sex with this guy.

"I don't really believe in pheromones," I said. "But I have no other way to explain it."

"Oh, I totally believe in pheromones. Haven't you ever been around someone that you're attracted to and you don't know why?"

I thought about it. No, I thought. I know why I'm attracted to someone. It's always something. It doesn't have to be rational. But I always know why.

"You know how I knew Sarah was into me?" he said gesturing to his wife at the other end of the couch. "We met each other at a funeral. This was when I was working out a ton. I was totally ripped. She wouldn't stop touching me. She was talking about how busy she was all the time. I just handed her my number and said 'call me when you're not busy'."

I must have looked unconvinced. Touching was a kind of visual cue, after all. Pheromones were an olfactory cue. This anecdote didn't prove anything.

Donald went on. He described a study where the scientists had men work out on treadmills until they were dripping with sweat. They took the men's sweaty shirts and put them in sealed jars. Then they had a young woman smell the shirts and rate them on a scale from one to ten on "attractiveness." The shirt that she rated lowest, that had made her gag upon smelling it, turned out to be her father's shirt. This was supposed to prove that pheromones signal to offspring that specific males are off limits, sexually speaking. If it were true, it could mean that much of our behavior is not necessarily pre-ordained but out of our conscious control.

I thought the subject needed further investigation. Maybe I didn't even know what pheromones were.

Later, after the conversation with Donald, I got online and started researching pheromones—because if the cause wasn't estrogen, maybe it was pheromones?

Fun Facts about Pheromones

1. Pigs are used to sniff out truffles because truffles emit an odor very similar to pig sex pheromones.

2. Estrogen, although not a pheromone, is the oldest hormone on the planet.

3. Although testosterone is often given to postmenopausal women to increase sex drive, our bodies can synthesize testosterone from estrogen and so the efficacy of this treatment is in question.

4. Humans as a species are much more susceptible to visual cues as opposed to olfactory cues. I wonder what dating is like for blind people. I once dated a man with no sense of smell. As far as I can tell this had no effect on our sex life.

5. Women's periods probably don't sync for pheromonal reasons, if at all. This effect, that women who live together sync their menstrual periods, is known as the McClintock effect and the study which produced this term has been impossible to reproduce. This effect is probably just a result of the variability of women's periods in general, and if they live together their periods will inevitably overlap to some degree. I can back this up with personal experience. I have six sisters and our periods were never synced for any real length of time. Thank God.

6. As it turns out, there isn't much scientific evidence for pheromones in humans after all. Their existence and the role they play in mating in humans is contested within the scientific communities. Every article I read seemed to doubt their existence as a factor in sexual attraction and behavior. I was surprised then, that they had somehow found their way so completely into our everyday conversations. Maybe it was because people had been mistaking pheromones for hormones. Hormones affect an individual's own behavior, not the behavior of others. Pheromones are chemicals secreted by the body that affect the behavior of others. Somehow it's easier to blame pheromones than it is to blame hormones, I guess. Easier to blame someone else, than to blame ourselves.

7. The results from many pheromone studies, like the one Donald told me about, cannot be reproduced. Or if they are reproduced the results are of no statistical significance.

I have to admit I was a little disappointed that pheromones were pretty much useless in explaining my behavior. I emerged from my bedroom and went out to the living room where my brother, my sister-in-law, my parents and my sister-in-law's mother were all watching the Miss America Pageant on TV.

I told them it pained me to see so many fake blondes on screen. "I'm a natural blonde," I said, "and all these women have such obviously fake blonde hair...it's just kind of annoying."

"Well, they're doing something right," my dad said.

"What do you mean?"

"Well it's a strategy that seems to work."

"Yeah. Right," I said.

I wondered if watching the Miss America Pageant was the best thing for me to be doing at that moment. Watching one Barbie doll after another parade across the screen in their bathing suits was just depressing me further.

We had the sound off on the TV. As the contestants came out in formal wear we started critiquing each gown. Raeann, my brother's mother-in-law, is a biologist and so I started sharing with her some of my new sexual selection fun facts.

"Well, it's been proven that symmetrical faces are more attractive," she said, her face perking up at the mention of science.

"I just learned something new today," I went on. "The reason, supposedly that we are attracted to symmetrical faces is that it's supposed to demonstrate how an organism can maintain symmetry while developing under stressors."

My sister-in-law scrunched up her face, "Well, I don't think that's true for me. I am usually attracted to people with unusual faces. Or what about those Japanese flower arrangements that are lopsided?"

"Well, there's also been studies that show that animals are attracted to novelty, because these traits strengthen the gene pool," I replied confidently. "You have to let new physical traits into the gene pool, otherwise things get too inbred."

Even in saying it, I knew my reply was too pat an answer. In this line of thinking everything had a biological reason. It implied that we're all just genetically pre-programmed robots.

Of course I knew this couldn't be true—after all my research, I still wasn't any closer to a biological answer to my question. I thought back to that first date at the Chinese restaurant. How he'd told me that I looked nice. I realized that there *had* been a line in the sand after all. I had made the decision to have sex with him. I'd made the decision right then and there.

You see, I'd broken up with my ex-boyfriend a year, almost to the day, before this date and when I'd sat on our couch weeping, my ex-boyfriend had told me the reason we weren't having sex was because he wasn't attracted to me anymore.

And so through gritted teeth, I'd told him that we should break up. I was too proud to say anything else.

I'd spent the next year slowly re-assembling my self-esteem. A whole year marked by bouts of depression and joy—a whole year—before walking into that Chinese restaurant, indulging in long navel-gazing sessions of regret and bitterness. So, sitting there at the table in my black dress and push-up bra, I must have looked like low-hanging fruit.

What I mean to say is that I must have looked desperate, even to myself. Because what I'd really done is spent a whole year trying to deny that I'd let one person so completely destroy my self-confidence, that I'd let another person have that much control over me. Instead of facing this, I'd pretended to be fine. That was it.

Pheromones don't exist. There's no mysterious biological factor controlling our actions and desires. Other people do have control over me but in a way I hadn't let myself believe. All this talk of pheromones, hormones and animal behavior was just a smoke screen.

What had really happened was this: I'd done something that I wasn't proud of, that I regretted. Emotionally, I wasn't really ready to be vulnerable to another person, and so had chosen to have sex with someone I didn't really care about and then write about it and read about it in front of an audience as a way to make myself feel better. Even sadder is that I wasn't self-aware enough to even cop to it, so I had tried to blame it on my birth control pills or pheromones.

Someone I loved didn't want to have sex with me anymore and so I had sex with someone who wanted to have sex with me, but who didn't love me and who I didn't love.

We turned off the pageant that night. The next morning I heard that the Indian-American Miss

New York was the new Miss America. All those fake blondes—their strategy hadn't paid off after all. And this made me happy.

Tourists

Maura O'Connell

Last year, my husband and I visited Spokane, Washington. We booked two nights in a low-rise hotel located along the city's River Walk, and spent a full day walking along the river and all over the city.

For anyone who has never been to Spokane, the River Walk is a long, paved dedicated bicycle and pedestrian path that stretches for several miles in each direction, on both sides of the Spokane River. It has limited access areas and parking lots where a person can park a car and begin their walk or bike ride. As we walked, we approached one such access spot, with benches and a parking lot and some institutional-looking buildings.

Seated on one bench were two people: an elderly man possibly in his 70s, dressed in denim overalls and a plaid shirt, and a middle-aged woman with an old-fashioned pageboy haircut and out-of-date clothes. I remember thinking that they looked like they had stepped out of the 1950s. My husband and

I were walking briskly, so we gave them a polite nod and wave, and intended to pass them.

"Hi folks!" the old man called exuberantly.

"Hi," we replied and continued walking.

"Do y'all ever feed the marmots?" he asked. Well, that stopped me in my tracks. I erroneously understood that marmots lived only in high mountain areas, not along riverbanks. I noticed that he was holding a large bag of white bread.

"Marmots?" I asked. I held up my hands to show him how large marmots are. "Y'know, marmots are about this big." I thought perhaps he was confusing marmots with smaller rodents like packrats or even ground squirrels.

"Oh, we will be careful!" he said sincerely.

"No, no, they aren't dangerous," I replied, and decided not to pursue the conversation any further. If the guy was feeding packrats and thinking they were marmots, who was I to correct him?

I smiled and waved. "Well, have fun!"

My husband and I kept walking. The old man said "Bye!" The woman never said a word; she just stared at us with a serene, Mona Lisa expression.

We walked along the path perhaps another mile. One or two cyclists passed us, but otherwise we had the trail to ourselves. We arrived at a fork in the trail, where we could continue along the same side of the river, or cross a bicycle-pedestrian bridge and get to the side of the river where our hotel was located. We decided to cross the river, stepping onto the bicycle-pedestrian bridge.

The bridge was wide enough to have several benches for tired walkers. And seated on the bridge's first bench were the strange old fellow and his blonde companion.

"Hi folks!" he called to us, as if he had never seen us before. I was so shocked that I just stopped. I didn't see how they could have possibly gotten in front of us. They didn't walk or ride bicycles past us. And we hadn't seen any parking lot access areas since we had passed them. So driving to their current destination on the bridge didn't seem possible either. It was as if they had just teleported themselves to a new spot, ahead of our arrival. I stood there for a couple of seconds in stunned silence.

"We just saw you!" I finally sputtered. The old man looked surprised and he shook his head.

"No," he said. His blonde companion turned toward him.

"Yes," she said to him.

"How did you get here?" I asked. The old man looked uncomfortable.

"Oh, we walk along a different part of the river every time we come here." His response really didn't answer how they got in front of us. The woman continued to look at us with her serene expression. She offered no word of explanation.

A chill ran up my spine and I suddenly got the sense that these two were not at all what they appeared to be. The thought did pop into my mind that they were extraterrestrial visitors, crazy as that may sound to some people. I decided not to be too pushy with my questions. *Just let them be,* I thought. Whatever they were, they seemed harmless. So, I waved again and my husband and I continued walking.

"Have fun!" I said as we passed.

"OK, that was weird," my husband said when we were well past the couple.

"Yes it was!" I exclaimed. "And if we see them a third time, I'm gonna *know* that they are aliens!"

We stepped off the bridge without further incident. Instead of turning left to go directly back to the hotel, we turned right to walk through the Gonzaga University campus. It turns out that marmots do live along the riverbanks at Gonzaga University. Who knew? We saw several roly-poly marmots lounging along the edge of the asphalt bike path. People clearly had been feeding them; they were huge and showed no fear of anyone. Okay, I thought, so maybe those two strangers were just tourists from a rural area who enjoy wandering along the Spokane River banks—and feeding the marmots.

We walked until we were tired, then turned around and headed back to our hotel, a return walk of two or three miles. As we passed the pedestrian-bicycle bridge, we tried to see if the two strangers were still sitting on the bench. But the bridge had a slight arch that obscured our view. So we shrugged and said, "Well, that's that," and continued the walk back to our hotel.

We arrived at the back doorway of our hotel building, when I happened to glance down the River Walk pathway.

And guess who was standing further down the path, about fifteen feet ahead of us, flinging breadcrumbs at some unseen rodent? I grabbed my husband's arm.

"Look!" I whispered loudly and pointed to the odd couple. Curiosity had overridden my fear and I decided that maybe I would go talk to them. I wanted to try and figure out if they were extraterrestrials or not.

"Let's get inside!" my husband said, grabbing my arm. His suggestion was probably the smarter one.

So I followed him through the door, up the stairs and into our hotel room.

"Okay, that was really weird," we both agreed once we were safely in our room.

We rested for about 30 minutes then left the hotel to walk to a restaurant for dinner. The strange couple was gone, and we didn't see them again on our trip.

Untold Story #2

Peg Quinn

My thirteen-year-old brother had died ten months before a Thanksgiving when my parents drove to be with relatives out of state. Home alone, I woke in the night and saw what looked like colored Christmas tree lights moving away from my bed and passing through the door. I 'knew' it was my brother.

I didn't have a very good relationship with my parents, but when they returned, I was telling them this incident at the breakfast table. I watched color drain from Dad's face.

He asked what night it was.

Saturday.

The same night he couldn't sleep and was pacing the hall in my uncle's house. Turning at one end, he saw what looked like Christmas tree lights vanish through the wall and 'knew' it was his son.

The Ghost Show

Peter Schwartz

My first memory of my father is of us at Jones beach. We're in the ocean up to my chest and every time a wave comes he picks me up under my armpits so I rise above it. Safe.

Then when I'm ten we move from Manhattan to suburban New Jersey because my father no longer wishes to practice psychiatry. He begins abusing me methodically. I remember sessions where if I made any sound when he hit me, he'd hit me harder. That got pretty ugly. I suppose it made me sleepy and aimless. I didn't do much for the next twenty years. I read a lot, wrote some poetry.

One day I started playing with the Paint program that comes with Microsoft Windows. I have O.C.D. so I practiced constantly for months. Form, line, color, texture. My work was published online and in university journals. I became art editor for a flash fiction site called DOGZPLOT, then later for a multimedia site, Mad Hatters' Review. My painting 'Malaria' was included in the May 2009 issue of *The Rotarian* which has a circulation of over half a million readers and featured Bill Gates on the cover. In short, I got some swagger.

Next, I decided I wanted to have my work shown in a major gallery. I stayed up for three days straight emailing thousands of galleries (again, O.C.D.) and sure enough a few days later I was offered a spot in a group show at the Amsterdam Whitney Gallery in Chelsea. My mother, surprised that I had shown such ambition and a former aspiring artist herself, agreed to drive me and my paintings to New York City.

The show was packed. New people kept arriving. Champagne bottles popped as the buzz in my ears got louder. Three different local television networks interviewed me for shows on the Manhattan art scene. A college friend Robert who I'd been in a band with showed up. My boss Carol from Mad Hatters' Review did, too. I felt publicly loved for the first time in my life.

I was staring at my piece titled 'the ghost show' when my mother tapped me on the shoulder and told me that I might have an interested buyer. All this glory, starting with my first published poem until now, was great, but so far had only earned me a few hundred dollars. The thought of selling one of my paintings and entering the art world was pure adrenaline. My heart remembered it was a muscle.

An old man in a dark blue suit shook my hand and I made a nervous joke about a little birdie telling me he might be interested in buying some artwork. I don't remember any more of the conversation— just a vague, pulling feeling that I had seen this guy somewhere before. At some point he turned to me and asked: you don't know who I am, do you?

His question answered mine. It was my father. Or rather, a bone-thin, heavily-wrinkled, bent-over version of my dad. He'd aged so much in the past decade since I'd seen him last I didn't even recognize him. My own father.

Now what you have to understand is for years, during college and afterward, I'd sworn if I ever saw my dad again I would, without hesitation, beat the shit out of him for all the times he'd tortured me. This thought had gone all the way into my body because when I realized who he was, without any conscious thought or premeditated choice, my right arm raised like it was going to hit him. And then something even more surprising happened.

He flinched. The buzz in my ears stopped entirely. He began talking very quickly about how he had wanted to be a musician and how my mother studied art before nursing but how the real world had pressured them into choosing professions to make money, but I had done it—that I was a real, actual artist and could now accomplish anything, that I was living my dream and that that was everything.

At this point he began to howl. I'm not using the word "cry" because that's not what he was doing. A loud, intensely mournful animal sound poured from his throat as he ran from the gallery.

My mother walked after him, presumably to console him. And I stood there. I just stood there. As ancient as anything on the planet. I stood there. Melting slightly, but widening, widening and widening and widening. With my art just as proudly and safely on the walls. I stood there. Shining like this was the most alive anyone could ever be. I stood there. Like a caveman in the future or maybe just a kid again. I stood there. Not aging, needing nothing, surrounded by art and possibilities. I stood there. Withstanding wave after wave after wave, laughing like a new voice that knows it will always be heard. I stood there. I stood there. I stood there until a young couple told me they just loved one of my black-and-white pieces titled 'wings of garbage'. Maybe they bought the one print I sold.

I don't know. I never bothered to ask. I thanked them. We might have even hugged. I know I shook his hand. I excused myself. Then got myself a glass of champagne.

Dellwood Drive

Chuck Howe

January 23, 1993
We are now all moved in. Everything looks good, but I have to remember to ask the landlord about getting into the attic. There have been noises up there all day. An animal must have gotten up there and I have no idea how to get in. Other than that, the move went well. Everyone is getting settled, even Ophelia. She likes the house, but she sits and barks at the front door all day, even though there is no one there. Hopefully that stops soon.

January 26, 1993
According to the landlord, there is no attic. At least there is no access to one, so whatever is living up there is here for the winter. Luckily it's not too bad. No worse than the other housemates. He also told me that we would probably want to keep the heat pretty low. It's gas heat, but for some reason, it seems to get expensive every year. Luckily it isn't too cold, and we all like to keep it pretty low anyway.

January 27, 1993
Ophelia is still barking at the front door non-stop. She has somehow figured out how to open the screen door now. Luckily can't unlock the front door, or else I am sure she would be out exploring the neighborhood.

Someone left the water running in the downstairs bathroom sink all night. I haven't heard anything about a water bill, but I am sure we will be charged for that at some point. Housemates. Can't live with them, can't afford the rent without them.

January 30, 1993
Either Carlos or Lauren keeps messing with the thermostat. We all agreed that the house should be kept at 72, but every time I look at it, the heat is set to 80. The house is badly insulated so there are drafts everywhere. Someone's room must get cold and they turn it up. I have to find out who. We were already warned that the gas bill gets high. If we keep it at 80, things are going to get really expensive.

February 1, 1993
Something weird happened today. We always thought that it was Ophelia opening the screen door, but she was out with Carlos all day, and I had to shut the screen door three times. No one came in or out, and I am absolutely sure that I latched it, at least I know that I did the last two times. I have no idea how it happened. Ophelia opening the door made sense. It's a bar handle and she jumps up on it.

February 2, 1993

Something keeps running across the roof or in the attic or something, and it's getting bigger and louder. Ophelia doesn't seem to hear it, she just keeps barking at the front door. I haven't even been here two weeks, and I am getting a weird vibe.

February 5, 1993

Carlos came running into the living room this morning as white as a sheet. He said when he woke up someone was standing over his bed. The person ran out into the hall when Carlos saw him. We were all in the living room, right at the other end of the hall. No one came running out of the hallway. Carlos must have been dreaming.

February 8, 1993

I came home today to find the front door wide open, and Ophelia gone. She was at a neighbor's house, they were looking after her. Lauren was the last one to leave and she swears she locked the door. I believe her. She's the one who is always most worried about locking the door. Maybe the landlord came by? But he would have locked up for sure. I did a quick look around, and nothing seemed to be missing.

February 10, 1993

I woke up drenched in sweat today. When I went and looked at the thermostat, it was set to 95 degrees. I yelled and screamed at everyone. Of course, they all said it wasn't them. What the fuck is wrong with these people?

February 12, 1993
Lauren keeps telling us that she senses a presence. Normally I'd laugh about it and ridicule her, but a lot of weird shit goes on in this place. Today the thermostat was set to 60. Is it just one of my housemates being an asshole and messing with us? Or is something going on here?

February 13, 1993
We were all woken up by the loud banging on the front door late last night. No one was there. No one was out on the street. If it was a kid doing a ring-and-run, he was a real professional. Shit is getting weird around here.

February 16, 1993
Carlos was woken up by the man standing over his bed again this morning. Is our housemate on drugs? Or drinking more than I realized? This time none of us were up or in the living room. The poor guy thinks he's going crazy, and he may be.

February 18, 1993
Lauren's friend, Jenna, came over today. She had to leave almost as soon as she got here. She said there was a bad man here. She wasn't looking at any of us when she said it, but we knew she wasn't talking about any of us. No one had told her anything about what has been going on.

Ophelia tried to leave with her. She has been very quiet lately. She doesn't bark at the front door anymore, but she watches it constantly.

February 21, 1993

What, is Lauren stupid? Why the hell would she bring a Ouija board into the house? Of course it said there was a monster living here that wanted to kill us all. Sure, ignoring it and hoping it will go away hasn't been working, but a Ouija board? Next she'll want to hire the short woman from *Poltergeist*.

February 22, 1993

I'll admit it. I was a little drunk. But drunk never made me see shit like that before. I was taking a piss in the downstairs bathroom when the door suddenly opened. I thought that I had locked it, but I was just zipping up and I figured it was just Ophelia barging in like she always does, now that she has learned to open doors.

When I turned and looked, it wasn't Ophelia. It wasn't anything really, just a white fog. It flowed quickly into the bathroom and then just disappeared. There was no shape or form to it. It was just a fog. I washed my face off, as if maybe it was something in my eye. But I couldn't comprehend what I had just seen.

I joined the others in the living room and tried to keep it to myself. Carlos could immediately tell something was wrong. Soon everyone was asking, so I told them. I had seen a ghost. I expected them to laugh at me, but no one did. They all just got quiet. I explained that it wasn't like the man that Carlos had seen. It was just a mist, and they all shook their heads, like they had all seen it before too.

March 2, 1993

Lauren and I are the last two left in the house. We just found a place across town and are moving next week. Whenever either of us is home alone, we hear conversations. Carlos took Ophelia with him when he moved out, but I still hear her running all over the place. The landlord wasn't surprised when we told him we were all moving out. He said that he has been "having a hard time keeping a tenant since Brian killed himself."

He wasn't going to tell me anymore, until I pressed him further. Brian and his girlfriend had rented the house five years earlier. They broke up. Brian got arrested for something, the landlord didn't go into detail, but Brian killed himself in jail. All of his stuff was still in the house, and the landlord ended up having to throw most of it away because no one had come to collect any of it. I never believed in ghosts before, but that does explain a lot of what had been going on here since we moved in. Luckily the landlord is letting us out of the lease, and Lauren and I can move in to our next place in just a few days. I want to get out of here immediately!

Before I went to bed tonight, I tried to talk to Brian. I told him that we would be out of the house soon, and then he would have it to himself again. Hopefully we have a peaceful last few days here.

1975

Ron Kolm

It's starting to snow. Nothing is sticking to the highway, but tiny wind-driven drifts scatter back and forth in front of the pickup truck as I drive to work. A winter storm has been predicted all day, but it hadn't started yet when I pulled out of the driveway.

I probably should have called in sick. I hate the damn job—night-shift on an assembly-line—which seems to be killing me in some way or another, but I need the money so I keep showing up and punching in, waiting for something to happen, an accident—anything—looking for a sign that I should quit and move on, but not finding any.

The snow gives me just the excuse I need to go back home; it will probably be a blizzard for sure, and I don't want to get snowed in at the plant—the idea of living on candy bars and cokes from the vending machines until we get rescued isn't a turn-on—I'm having enough problems with my marriage as it is, and that would only make matters worse, so I turn left off the bypass onto a side road where I can do a U-turn and return to the rundown farmhouse my wife and I live in.

The secondary road I'm now on is very steep, dropping away from the bypass at an extreme angle, and it's much higher in the middle than on the shoulders. After I turn around and start driving back up toward the highway, my truck shifts to the right, sliding on the fresh snow, until it slams into the curb. Nothing I do can budge it. I try the old trick of shifting into third gear and then slowly giving it some gas, but that doesn't work—I guess the grade is just too much for my old pickup truck with its under-powered six-cylinder engine.

I turn off the car radio and switch off the ignition, and sit there, considering my options. The only one I can come up with is to leave my truck and walk up to the roadside and try to flag down a passing driver and hitch a ride home, but there were almost no cars on the highway when I turned off it. A kind of pall descends over me, a sort of numbness. I live more than a couple of miles away, too far to walk in the worsening storm, so I sit there, in a complete stasis, watching the falling snow coat the windshield. And then I hear a shout.

I look out the window, then roll it down, white flakes landing on my left knee. Idling beside me is a very peculiar vehicle—a pure white World War II vintage jeep with the words 'Borough of Mt. Penn' stenciled in black letters on its side. The guy sitting in the passenger seat asks me if I need help and when I say, "yeah," he takes a couple of handfuls of rock salt from a bag that seems to be on his lap and tosses them out of his open window in such a way that they land under the wheels of my truck. I know how strange this sounds, but I swear that this is what I see. I turn the key and my pickup comes back to life. I steer the front wheels slightly to the left, gently pumping the gas pedal, and it moves forward, almost as if by magic. The guys in the jeep wave at me as they speed off, and I drive up to the top of the hill and turn right, heading home, as the snow continues to fall.

I park the truck in the driveway, walk through a couple of inches of the white stuff, and go into the house. The cat, at least, seems happy to see me back—he probably figures there's food in his immediate future. I unlace my wet work shoes and toss them down the steep stairway that leads to the kitchen, scaring the cat—I'll open a can of tuna for him later.

I sink back into our beat-up sofa in the living-room, and exhale deeply, relieved to finally be home. I still can't wrap my head around what happened out there—it was like some kind of minor miracle—the image of the guy throwing rock salt under my tires is still so vivid, even though it was snowing heavily when it happened. It was like some kind of strange mid-day sun was shining down on everything, erasing the storm; it all seems so bright in retrospect.

Like the good husband I'm still trying to be, I know I should call my wife at her shitty part-time job at the health food store, and tell her I've bailed out on going to work. I pick-up the phone, look for the store number on a piece of paper scotch-taped to it, and dial.

Her manager answers, and, gritting my teeth, I ask if I can speak to my wife. I know the guy is hitting on her, because she's made a point of telling me. Just another reason to love my life. He puts me on hold. I wait a while, and she finally picks up.

"What do you want, Ronnie? You know I'm at

work, and they don't like it when I get personal calls."

"Well, it's snowing pretty hard now, so I turned around and came back home...didn't want to get stuck in the plant overnight. They said it might be seven or eight inches...."

"Big deal! I'm gonna stay and finish my shift. Besides, you know I'm going to a party after work—you're just trying to mess up my evening!"

"No, really," I say, trying to defuse the bomb in the room. "It might get pretty bad—I can pick you up after work..."

"My cousin is giving me a ride—you know that. Really, Ronnie, I have to get back to work. Goodbye."

"Okay...bye," I say, putting the phone back on the receiver. I look at the cat who's looking at me. "Jeez," I say to him, "I am so fucked...."

I put a record on the turntable—Jimi Hendrix—and lean back against the cushions. I really have no idea what to do with myself. At least fighting with my wife wasn't boring, but I sure am bored now.

I look out the window at the falling snow, but my mind stays blank. And then it hits me—I know what I can do to get through the rest of the day—I'll do some drugs—always a great way to collapse time. I have a stash of stuff our friends have given us over the years; stuff we haven't gotten around to using, or stuff we're still kind of afraid to try. There's even some stuff in the small box that's a total mystery—I have a friend in California who sends me pills in every letter he mails me—I have no idea what they are, or what they do. I head to the closet and reach behind a stack of sweaters and pull out the stash box. Then I go back to the sofa with it to check everything out.

The box has some weed in it; I know what that is, and some mushrooms.

My wife has pretty much stopped doing drugs, and I only smoke marijuana when I listen to music before hitting the sack. But I want something stronger; not a lot stronger, but something to put me in a different space, a better one. Everything looks different than I remember. I check out the pills. I'm pretty sure some of them might be acid, which I still haven't done, but one of them is supposed to be mescaline, which I have done, and which took me on a pretty nice trip. So I opt for the mescaline, and swallow the rather tiny black pill. Without water. Then back to Hendrix.

But I've made a mistake; the pill I've taken is not mescaline—it turns out to be acid, or so I guess as my world goes somewhere else. I see hideous angels outside the windows, banging on the glass, trying to get in. Everything is moving and breathing.

I watch my cat tearing back and forth across the room; he must know something is awry. I want to play with him; heck, I want to *be* like him—I want to express my inner cat—so I get down on all fours and start prowling around on the floor beside him, which really spooks him out. He starts clawing at the plants we have on either side of the couch. I tear at them, too. We really fuck with them. Somewhere in the back of my mind I know my wife isn't going to like this adventure I'm having. Then the cat goes over to his kitty-litter and pees and then covers the piss. I don't have to pee, but I run my fingers through the gray gravel as if I had. The cat is absolutely wide-eyed in disbelief.

My personality begins to peel away as if I'm an onion; layer after layer. Memories flash by and then disappear. When I get to what seems to be the very core of my being I freak out; there isn't anything there I recognize. I simply can't handle what I'm going through. I try calling friends to ask for help, but no one's home. Or perhaps I'm using the phone wrong. I finally manage to call the health food store again, and eventually my wife gets on the phone:

"Ronnie, what the hell do you want? Why are you doing this to me? I have to get off the phone—right now!"

"But, honey, I think I just dropped some acid... something like that...I'm really fucked up..."

"I don't care! You're just doing this to piss me off!"

"Please, dear, please let me pick you up. I'll take you anywhere you want to go. I think I need help..."

"Okay, I'll leave work and start walking along the bypass. It's probably still snowing. This really sucks, Ronnie!"

She hangs up the phone, and then I do too, looking at it for a long while. Maybe it's only a couple of minutes, though it seems like hours—then I get a pair of slippers from the closet and put my coat on, and head out the front door to my truck. I'm still quite high, but things have leveled off to a degree where I can sort of function, though mostly in a reactive way. It's like I'm outside of myself watching me go through the motions.

It's now evening, and the snow has stopped falling—there's almost a foot of it—and my slippers are soaked by the time I get into the truck. I turn on the engine and back out of the driveway, glad I have a pickup and not a regular car. Our road hasn't been plowed yet, but my vehicle handles it just fine. I figure I'll head down the hill and drive through the center of Reading and then get on the bypass on the other side of town.

When I hit the city limits I see the most incredible things: cars that have crashed into each other, cars that skidded into snowbanks, cars up on the sidewalks, people yelling at each other. All the stoplights in my direction are blinking yellow, and I seem to be gliding by everything without effect. I don't have to stop once. It's as if I'm watching a film, and everything is one long traveling shot; no edits, no problems. I am there and not there; I am driving, but I'm also the passenger. Other than observing the scenery as it rolls past, I only have one idea in mind: I have to find my wife.

I merge onto the bypass. It's very dark, and the roads are slippery, but there is no other traffic. My headlights illuminate the road in front of me, and a little bit of the shoulder. And then I see her, framed in the light, struggling through the snowdrifts on the side of the highway.

I am amazed at my good luck, but I also sort of take it for granted, too. It is all part of the magic that started so much earlier in the day when I decided not to go to work. The fact that we're out in the middle of nowhere doesn't even enter into my thinking.

I stop and pop open the door on the passenger side and, grinning, tell her to hop in—in my movie this is where the lovers are about to be reunited—but not in hers...

"You fucking asshole, Ronnie! What is wrong with you?"

And I can't wipe the smile off my stupid face. It has become a rictus. I'm the Joker, powerless to change my expression. I want to cry, to shout; yet I sit there frozen, helplessly grinning.

"Take me to the bowling alley at the shopping center, and then go home. I told my cousin to meet me there. What's wrong with you anyway?"

"Um, I took some acid by mistake...I was bored..."

"You really are an idiot! Well, I guess you can

still drive—get me to the bowling alley—you know where it is."

Which I do, somehow. When we get there we both get out of the truck and stand behind it to say our goodbyes. The white back-up lights are on; I must have parked in reverse; the engine is idling and exhaust is trailing up from the tail pipe, which is vibrating slightly. All of my powers of concentration are focused on that one point—condensation is dripping out the end of it and splattering, ever so slightly, on bare asphalt; most of the parking lot had been plowed before we got there; high mounds of snow surround us.

I keep looking down, lost, and my wife finally says, "Okay, let's go home—I'll drive." And our relationship continues on a little while longer.

The Right Card

Gay Degani

It started in the summers in Louisiana where it's always hot—rain-wet without the rain. Inside, laughing and smoking adults would sit at card tables in the enclosed back porch where boxy air conditioners blew icicles, while I ran barefoot on crushed shell streets with cousins, playing Superman and other such things. I had a lot of relatives on Dunn Street, families with five to eight kids. I was from California. I was an only child.

Friends and kinfolk were always crowding around my grandma's stove sampling jambalaya, drinking beer, or sitting at the dining room eating red fish and gumbo. After cookies and jellyroll, they'd wander through my mom's childhood bedroom or the kitchen and into my grandparents' room, then out the door at the foot of their bed onto the converted back porch to play Canasta, Pokeno, Yahtzee, or Liverpool Rummy.

It was a sunroom really, with light streaming in its long back wall of windows. My grandma's white wicker furniture was on one side while on the far end sat a small black and white TV on a metal stand. In the middle there was enough room for two small or one large round card table depending on the game we were playing. My grandpa, who was handy with a saw, made the circular table topper out of plywood and my grandma whipped up a flannel cover held in place with elastic. To me, an only child, that sunny room, bursting with warm and affable relatives, was magic.

I don't remember who was there when it happened. My mom, dad, grandparents, a cousin or two, a friend, air conditioner on freezing, refrigerator stocked with orange and grape soda, Coca-Cola, Seven-Up, the promise of watermelon later out on the patio, iced down in galvanized tubs.

The goal of most of the games we played had to do with making sets in our hands so we could lay down our cards and go out. Least amount of points won. Sets consisted of three or more of a kind, i.e. all sixes, tens, queens), or three or more in the same suit forming a straight, for example a 2, 3, 4 of hearts or 10, jack, queen of clubs. Each player took turns pulling from the deck of cards left over from the deal, always hoping his or her draw would be the right card to complete a set.

I don't remember exactly which game it was, but that doesn't matter. What matters is what happened. I'd been playing along, doing well, getting intense about winning. At first, all I did was *think* about the card I needed when I drew and surprise, surprise, I got it! I grinned. On my next turn, I concentrated harder, eyes closed. Pulled a card. Boom! Another good one. I hadn't thought the trick could work twice in a row. Would it, *could* it happen a third time?

I shut my eyes, pictured the card, opened my eyes, held my hand over the stack, and wriggled my fingers. I felt an electric pulse buzz between my fingers and the stack of cards. I looked around, wondering if anyone else knew what was happening, that I was talking to the card inside my head, asking it to morph into the card I wanted.

Someone blew out a long stream of smoke. Slowly, I peeled the top card off the stack. And WOW! It worked, and as I remember it all these years later, it seemed to happen again and again.

But did it really happen? I don't know. Maybe not. Did it happen more than just that one day? I believe it did, at least for a couple of summers, but of course, too soon, I grew out of childhood and into "reality." I began to accept that there is no such thing as magic, and later, no such thing as prayer, because that's what it was, this magic: a kind of prayer. Eventually I accepted that although we might wish for the ability to appeal to a higher being or to the universe for help or guidance, for the most part, we are on our own.

Yet. Yet. There have been so many other times when I've felt a very real connection with something out there, something I could call upon to work *with* me, if I could only invoke that charge—that pulse I felt when playing cards.

What proof do I have of this? Nothing big. Small bits of evidence come at me unexpectedly, how I pick up one random book-on-CD in the library and then select a second one that on the surface seems to have nothing to do with the first, but when I listen to them, I recognize similar patterns in theme or a juxtaposition in setting, a correlation that ups the ante on my understanding of something deeper. Perhaps I tap into primal thoughts, not fully realizing I seem to know instinctively some truth or some approach. As a writer, these revelations are as essential to my craft as is the faith that what I want to say will eventually come to me. I will get it right. Like the card in Liverpool Rummy, the right idea, the right twist, the little revelation will magically be there.

Believe

Ben Tanzer

The public record does not reflect that two historically significant events occurred in the spring/summer of 1986.

First, I lost my virginity at a friend's house during my second attempt at doing so. The first attempt had been less than successful, the lack of belief in my ability to perform dooming the whole operation to failure before it ever began.

Second, and shortly thereafter, while at the Vestal Drive-In, in a similarly compromising position in the back of my parents' blue station wagon, I took a moment to look out the window and I saw a UFO.

The facts of these events have always been beyond dispute as far as I'm concerned, but there's been no official recognition of either event until now.

Why is this?

In terms of my virginity, and loss thereof, it is my understanding that there is no body tasked by law with tracking the sexual exploits of a single teenage boy. Not that the government has admitted to anyway. And certainly not since John Hughes died.

However, regarding my UFO—and yes it is mine—while I'm certain that there is a top-secret agency somewhere that is quite aware of every UFO sighting everywhere, even mine, I am also certain that the sweaty, nearsighted analyst who knows about my presence at the Vestal Drive-In on that night is not allowed to officially report on the details of the evening.

But I am.

I imagine that sex and UFOs, and by extension, sex and space, and by further extension, sex and what we now think of as nerd culture, are rarely considered in the same breath, much less the same free association, much less conflated to the point where they are intertwined and quasi-dependent on one another.

But hear me out.

Space, like UFO sightings, is about infinite possibility, if not an actual rupture of one's consciousness, though the presence of UFOs more specifically represent not just space and the vast unexplored opportunities contained therein, but the possibility that somewhere in the universe there is intelligent life, and someone, or something, besides us, which exists, hence ensuring that the chance of us making a connection with someone, or something, is far greater than we could have believed.

By this definition then, sex is of a similar ilk, and yet completely not so at all.

At its best, sex promises at least a moment of connection where none may have previously existed, but unlike space where the possibilities are endless, sex for most—some—is clouded by the lack of opportunity, or the belief that the opportunity to find it is fleeting. Present, then gone, briefly floating there before you like a UFO, ethereal and glowing, and yet just beyond your reach, unless you, they, us, me, happen to be in the right place, and looking in the right direction, at the right time.

It is luck, and to some extent, available to you because you have been chosen based on some series of calculations you can't quite grasp.

Or, as my mother might say, maybe that's just me.

It's important to note, not that it isn't obvious by now, that I was obsessed with space, though more specifically science fiction—it wasn't the stars I cared about, it was the people populating them—long before I was obsessed with sex.

It began with Star Wars, but doesn't everything?

And no, you don't need to answer that, I know it does.

To be clear, it's not that my obsession with sex, or even science fiction, starts with Star Wars exactly, but the idea of obsession as a thing or a life force, and the feeling of wanting to experience something so badly that you're willing to consume it, and even destroy it, certainly did.

It's about wanting something all the time.

It's also about not being able to think about anything else.

That was Star Wars for me. It was new and different, and a manifestation of all the things I was already obsessing about: space, escape, heroism, fathers, and I suppose sex as well, even if I didn't quite get that yet.

Close Encounters of the Third Kind would soon grab me in a similar fashion. It dared me to believe that there was something bigger out there and unexplained, and that whatever it was, it was worth chasing because it spoke to the possibility that maybe things could be explained, and if that was possible, then Little League and rich kids didn't have to have so much power over me, and the world didn't have to be so confusing.

In 2015 all of this is somehow cool. People want to talk about the X-Men or Star Trek, or at least go to the movies like Star Wars so they can talk about them if they have to. But back then—and I don't care how successful Star Wars was—that wasn't the case. None of it was cool, and for a moment, that was fine with me.

It is now 1986 and N., so very not her actual initial, announced in the school cafeteria that she *would* sleep with me before I graduated. When this information reached me in the way these things do, someone told someone who told someone who told me, I made a beeline for N.

I didn't have to ask anything but, "When and where?"

We agreed to meet at my house the next day after track practice.

It did not go so well.

In retrospect, should I have jerked-off right before she came over in an effort to prevent premature ejaculation?

Maybe not.

But should I have a second time to be safe?

Definitely not.

Still we worked it out just weeks later and then I asked her to go to the drive-in with me.

We were in the back of the station wagon, and I know you are supposed to keep your eyes closed, because that's what a friend had told me, and possibly a character played by Molly Ringwald, but I didn't. I liked to watch, and as I shifted into some kind of compromising position, the night is so very dark, the moon a million miles away, and, because we didn't go to the actual drive-in, but instead parked behind it, it was so quiet, and there were no distractions, it was just us, only us, and I looked out the window and there it was, a ship of some kind, off above the car, hovering for a moment, glowing and cylindrical. I locked on to it, and I looked for any signs that would make it anything but a UFO—numbers, logos, wings or a tail, a cockpit—but there wasn't anything. It was a UFO, which I watched until it moved away, and then I lingered there for a moment, awaiting its return...something, anything, but there was nothing. It was ephemeral, and now it was just me and N. again, alone, the two of us, and nothing else.

The next day the newspaper reported the sighting and went on to say that there were no military planes or weather balloons in the area that night.

Not that I can find any reference to that article now.

Regardless, there was no formal explanation for what I saw.

One explanation not reported, however, is that I saw the UFO because I was finally having sex, that it was a manifestation of what was going on for me internally, a break with consciousness and the desperation I felt, which manifested itself in access to not just a new world, but all worlds, the one we live in, the ones out there, parallel worlds, all of them.

All of which would be cool, and may even be true—at least I choose to believe that's a possibility anyway. But I also have to recognize how the UFO appeared to me as my childhood fascination, and obsession, with space, and all things science fiction was passing.

The question for me now, is whether I had truly eschewed all of that as a means for fitting in and getting laid, or had I merely outgrown it?

Was the UFO a message from something larger than me, and what I could actually grasp at the time, thus, maybe not a break with consciousness, but a break with who I had been up until that point, now lost to space and youth?

Also, who the fuck do I think I am asking these questions in the first place?

Richard Linklater?

"I never got Star Wars," D., so totally the correct initial, said the night I met her.

It was 1987 and I had been drawn to her legs and long brown hair, but it was the fates, and our roommates locking the door to my dorm room to have sex, that pushed us together and led to us talking all night about our mutual love for *Days of Our Lives* and *Soap*, the show, not the product, and her inexplicable preference for the clearly second rate and derivative *Knot's Landing* over *Dallas*.

Still, while there was connection, and alchemy, D. said she didn't get Star Wars.

It didn't really mean anything to me at that point, and besides, eventually sleeping with her was all that really did matter. But it had once, and *Dallas* was one thing, but could I be with someone who didn't like Star Wars?

Apparently I could and apparently I had crossed over to the dark side myself, because later I decided to ask D. to marry me.

It was now 1994, and not a great year for science fiction movies at all, except for *Star Trek: Generations*, maybe, which to be honest, I didn't even go to see.

We were driving cross country, D. and I, and I had been desperately carrying an engagement ring with me for days, hoping for the right moment to propose.

But there wasn't a right moment, or I wasn't ready, or something, and so as we were driving through Wyoming, dodging Bison, and torrential rains, I committed myself to asking the next day no matter what.

What didn't initially occur to me is that our plan had already been to camp outside of Devil's Tower, the location of the climactic finale to *Close Encounters of the Third Kind*.

What could be more perfect?

We pulled into the campsite late at night, it was dark and impossible to see much of anything, much less Devil's Tower itself. However, there was one thing we could see very well, there was a sheet stretched between two trees and they were showing *Close Encounters of the Third Kind*.

Boom.

Magic.

Karma.

Something.

Everything.

"Oh, my God, look," I said to D.

She looks.

"Ughhh, is that *Close Encounters*? I hate that movie," D. replied.

Did this give me pause?

It did.

Of course, I had been pausing for days now.

I was done pausing.

I asked D. to marry the next morning at the base of Devil's Tower.

D. and I do not talk about Star Wars or UFOs, and she never dug *X-Files*, but that's been okay, we've had *The Sopranos*, bills to pay, trips to Los Angeles, co-workers to complain about and doughnuts to eat.

Two things have changed though, and while not as profound as losing my virginity or seeing a UFO, they have had a significant impact on what I am now, or at least how I live now.

First, the world has caught up with who I once was.

Second, D. and I had children, who love science fiction and superheroes.

They think it's fascinating that Luke and Leia are actually brother and sister. They want to argue about who would win a fight between the Incredible Hulk and Superman. They beg me to show them any scenes from *Game of Thrones* that involve dragons burning cities and tearing people in half.

And with every Marvel movie we go to together, and every time I skip work to watch *Mad Max: Fury Road* on opening night, or when I binge long into the night watching *Orphan Black* or *Daredevil* in a sweaty, joyous frenzy, I have come to recognize everything I gave up to become something else, and that not only can I be what I am now and that other person too, but how much I missed all of it.

I suppressed my desire to be a fanboy because I wanted to be cool.

But I want to dissect the storylines of *Game of Thrones* at work and understand where and how the show and books deviate. I want to attend the Chicago

Comic & Entertainment Expo and pose for pictures with people dressed-up as Spider-Man. And I want to believe that J.J. Abrams is going to get the new Star Wars movies right because he has to.

I have come home.

All that's truly missing is a return visit from my UFO.

It will be thirty years this summer since I last saw it, and it hasn't reappeared yet. But I'm ready, and I'm waiting, and I believe.

Again.

Why Am I Here?

Shawn Kilburn

Every year, around January, I begin to feel this creeping gloom and dread, regular as clockwork. For a long time I chalked it up to the dim winter light and cold, the long nights. I always assumed it was a coincidence that January is my birthday month. Now, I'm not so sure.

Sometimes I'm driving my kids to school or drinking coffee or strolling about the neighborhood and I start wondering, "Why am I here?" Not in an existential way, you understand. I'm actually wondering how I could possibly be here. You see, based on what I know about my birth, I shouldn't actually be here. I shouldn't have survived the story of my birth, and yet, here I am.

I've listened to the story of my birth probably hundreds of times. Sheer repetition has caused me to ignore the improbability of it all for a long time. It wasn't strange, because it was so familiar. Because it became familiar, I started telling people the story, almost as if I had been there myself. I mean, I was there, but I wasn't. It's difficult for me to tell the story in a thoughtful way, because it became so rote for so long. For no particular reason that I can identify, I've started pondering this story in a way I never have before.

My birthday is in January, but I should have been born in early April. I was born much too soon and with circumstances that should have ended things right there.

Let me back up. I'm trying to tell this story in a way that I haven't done before. It's so easy to fixate on the funny details, like the tipi or the goat. The funny details have always, for me anyway, helped obscure the intensity and struggle for survival, the darkness and fear, of that night.

My mom was hitchhiking and my dad picked her up. That's how they met. It was Santa Cruz. It was the 70s. They were hippies, I guess, at a time when that had stopped being cool. Except in little hippy enclaves, like the Santa Cruz mountains. I only remember my mom telling this story once. My dad never has. I was always both intrigued and repulsed hearing stories about the time before I was born. I have no idea if this is typical or not. I've always hated asking direct questions of people, instead preferring to infer meaning and story from hints and oblique comments.

I know that my dad was driving his truck. I know that my mom was hitchhiking. I know that my dad picked her up. I know that they hit it off and spent the weekend together. I know...actually, I don't know any of this. I only know this from what my mom has told me, a precarious knowing. Even now, the thought of asking her direct questions about this time makes me feel cold and tense. As I write this, I find my body hunched forward, curled slightly around my belly, right shoulder turned forward.

I don't know, but I can infer, that I was the result of that first meeting between my parents. I know nothing of what that discovery was like. I know nothing of the first conversation about that. I know nothing of those next several months. At some point, my parents moved in together. Right now, you're probably imagining two people moving into a house, maybe filled with hairy, dirty kids hanging out of windows. Maybe you're imagining a small apartment, a couch, some chairs, definitely a kitchen.

Imagine: a circle on the ground, perhaps 15-20 feet wide. Now stretch the edge of the circle up, up, like topographical clay, and in, until the edge of the circle shrinks into a point about 10-12 feet above. Now imagine that stretched edge is made of some kind of tough waterproof fabric, canvas maybe.

A tipi. (Or teepee, if you prefer). Yes, my parents lived in a tipi. It's like the punchline to a joke. I have to imagine that the tipi was set up on a wooden platform of some kind, for it to make any kind of long-term sense.

That in itself would be enough for a story, right? I've certainly never met anyone else who's lived in one. Let alone as any kind of long-term arrangement.

Other things I know about this time: My parents were squatting on some guy's land, rent free. My parents owned or took care of a goat. My mother apparently loved to do cartwheels and somersaults. My mother's son, my half-brother, lived with his dad. That Christmas before I was born, my mother made paper chain decorations. I don't think there was a tree. My mother really liked the mini-series, *Roots*, but couldn't watch it in the tipi without electricity.

Things I imagine, but don't know for sure: I imagine there were kerosene lamps and candles. I imagine that the floor of the tipi was covered in rugs, blankets, pillows. Maybe there was a chair or two. Maybe not. I imagine maybe a propane camp stove. I suspect that my imaginings are, despite my best efforts, influenced by pictures of the John Lennon/ Yoko Ono bed-in.

Over the years, my mother has had different ideas about why I was born early. The current theory involves the goat. Apparently, my parents had a goat. Or there was a goat that was around. One day shortly before I was born, my mom was walking the goat on a line. The goat bolted and, instead of letting go of the line, she held on, falling face first on the ground. I've been told my grandmother thought it had something to do with my mom's doing cartwheels and somersaults. Perhaps it was something else. They were hippies, after all.

Whatever the reason, on that cold January night, my mom, alone with my two-year-old brother, went into labor. Then I was born. I'm not sure how long they were there with me, before my dad came home from work. No telephone. I imagine my dad walking down a hill, walking slowly through the dark, maybe my mom was yelling, and then he started hurrying. I imagine him bursting into the tipi, witnessing all the messiness of birth. I imagine him running up the hill to his truck, his car, his what, I don't even know.

It's at this point in the story when I start to realize all the questions I didn't ask. What was it like running back up (?) the hill through the dark? What was it like fumbling with car keys in the dark? What was it like making that decision—to try and get my mom, my brother, and me to the car or to try and go for help? It can't have been easy, but, for me, he made the right one. Here I am. Typing this.

I don't know if he went for a telephone or if he went to the nearest bar to get help. Whatever he did, he found the only quasi-official rescue workers in that small mountain town: the part-time, unpaid volunteer firemen.

My mom said they were very professional when they arrived, although she could smell the beer on their breath, their beer-breath frosting in the cold January night. They bundled her, and me, and my brother up in a blanket, got them in a truck, and started driving down that twisty twisty mountain highway. Somewhere along the way, they met an ambulance. I recall my mom marveling at how calm and collected the volunteer firemen were compared to how freaked out the EMT was. He started unwrapping the blanket covering me and my mom, wanting to cut the umbilical cord (was it still uncut?), but she yelled at him and got in the ambulance. Apparently, there was some talk about a helicopter ride, but it was not to be.

Since, I've driven that mountain highway many times. It's a long 19 miles to the Santa Cruz city limits and then however long it is from there to the hospital. A long long drive in which I stayed alive. A long long drive to the hospital, where I had to live in an incubator, a warm box, to keep me alive for the next several weeks.

I have stamps of my tiny hands and feet. I have a photo of my dad holding my entire body in his two cupped hands. I have a photo of my mom looking down at me. Somehow, from that small self, I arrived at the person I am now. From less than three pounds I have grown and grown.

I grew and grew from something small. And so did you and you and you. Now that I have children of my own, I marvel at how they've grown, too, from things so small. From a thing you cannot even see to a thing that rolls and spins and shouts around a room.

So, yes, I wonder sometimes how that happened. Not how I came to be, but how I came to still be here. Because it seems like, somehow, somewhere on that dark cold road, that windy road of rock and stabbing pines, I should have ceased to be. I don't think there's some magical explanation. I don't think I have some deeper purpose in this life.

But I do try to live my life with care. Sometimes I remember why.

If the Wheat, the Sky, and the Clouds Could Talk

Julie Allen

When I was 12 years old I saw something that would begin a lifetime curiosity of the unexplained. I didn't tell anyone about that day in the field, and neither did my mom and brother, Jeff, who saw it, too. We kept quiet, mostly fearful that people would think we were crazy like all the others who came forward and told their stories. Finally, after 35 years, I'm ready to tell the story.

Our grandparents, Granny and Papa, lived in a small rural town on the Missouri river. It was a quiet place with a population of about 153. There wasn't much for us kids to do in this town. Sometimes we'd walk the railroad tracks by the river in hopes of seeing a huge sand barge stealthily making its way on its journey, or maybe see a threatening whirlpool suck in everything that floated by. On occasion, my oldest brother would take me hunting for Indian artifacts in the wheat fields by the river. After a healthy rain, treasures of tomahawks, pottery pieces and arrowheads from past lives would reveal themselves in the black soil. Other than the fun of walking the tracks, or hunting artifacts, having lunch with my grandparents every Sunday was the biggest treat of all. Granny would cook up a feast for anyone who showed up. When she didn't make her famous cheeseburgers or pot roast, Papa would surprise us all with Long John Silver's! We never knew what would be on the menu, but we always left with full bellies and warm thoughts of the day. However, there was one Sunday that would leave us with more than a full belly and more curious thoughts than we could imagine.

We'd just left our grandparents that summer day and Mom was driving the usual route home, a winding, country road down by the wheat fields and Missouri river. The windows were down, radio cranked on the local rock station and Mom, typically driving the speed of light. Jeff took shotgun, so I was left to be blown away by the hot wind in the back seat, barely able to hear the radio station, leaving my mind to daydream out the window.

We were heading up around a curve when something shiny caught my eye in the field ahead. As we got closer, possibly 900 yards away from it, I could see it was a metallic-looking object, hovering over the field. At first, I thought it might be a small passenger plane, which would not have been uncommon since there was an airport nearby. However, as we got closer I noticed it appeared to have an odd shape. Trying to focus on this object, I soon realized it was nothing I had ever seen before. Leaning up to the front seat, I asked Mom to slow down so I could get a better look at it. At this point, Jeff saw it too and yelled for Mom to stop the car. She quickly pulled over to the side of the road, brought the car to a screeching halt and turned off the engine. This thing now had Mom's undivided attention, too.

Dust floated around the car as we set there with fixed eyes on the field. All was quiet. It was if the world were void of sound except for the subtle chirping of birds nearby in the trees. We were quiet, too, gazing at this thing with mouths wide open, wondering what we were looking at. The hot sun beat down and reflected brightly off its surface, giving off a wavy heat-like haze all around it, distorting its image. It eerily hovered in one place about 500 feet from the ground, making no sound at all. After a while of watching this object, wondering what it would do next, it shifted, and appeared to dance and sway as if we were its audience and it knew we wanted a better look. Soon, the shape became apparent, but foreign. It was like all those people say; silver and disk shaped, with a small dome-like top. There were no apparent lights, no doors or windows.

"What is that?" Mom whispered, as if this object might hear her.

"Is that a UFO?" my brother whispered.

Realizing what Jeff said, Mom quickly snapped, "Stay in the car!"

We watched the object for what seemed like an eternity when it started gliding toward us, as if it were inspecting us, too. My heart began to race and curiosity quickly changed to fear. I looked to see if others were on the road with us, but we were alone with this thing.

I yelled for Mom to "GO!" as I wanted to get away from it.

My brother yelled for her to "STOP!" as his boyhood dreams of adventure were finally coming true.

As a way of sort of satisfying both our requests, with eyes still peeled toward the field, Mom slowly eased her foot onto the gas and started up the hill toward home. As we neared the top of the hill, the treetops became our shield from this object, though we could still see part of it and its slow dance over the field. Suddenly, as if bored with us, the thing shot strait up and then zipped diagonally out of site into the atmosphere leaving us in complete bewilderment. All of a sudden, I too was disappointed that it flew away and was sorry I made Mom drive away from it.

Not fulfilled with our experience, Mom quickly turned the car around and drove speedily back down the hill toward the field. Our eyes glued to the sky, hearts racing in anticipation of what we might see, Mom pulled over to the side of the road and stopped the car. We searched the sky one last time for this thing, thinking it might have flown back down to entertain us once again.

We sat mostly in quiet, with an occasional question that couldn't be answered; *what was this thing?* There was no answer for us. Only the wheat waving at us in the wind, the blue sky, and a few wispy clouds above.

If the wheat, the sky and the clouds could talk, they could probably tell us an amazing story. Instead, we were left to wonder, knowing that we were lucky enough to have had a brief encounter with *another* kind.

The Matching Key

Kelli Fuqua Hart, MA

I lost my great-grandmother, Ida Mae Fuqua, in 2006, when I was pregnant with my daughter. The events surrounding her death always weighed on me because for 27 years, my great-grandmother and I had been extremely close. Yet, the day she passed, unexpectedly, I couldn't have been much farther away, having just landed in San Diego, CA.

My great-grandmother was not sick. She was of sound mind and lived in the same home she had lived in with my great-grandfather for decades. There was no cause for concern that would have made me think my trip to California was at a bad time. However, only hours after landing, I learned of her passing, which happened peacefully in the midst of her afternoon nap.

I wasn't there to see her or be with her after they rushed her to the hospital, where they said she was still alive but, comatose, for only a brief moment before finally drawing her last breathe. I struggled for a few years knowing that I hadn't been there.

I spent one night in San Diego before flying back to Ocala to lay her to rest. I took solace by her side, said my "goodbyes" and asked her to stay with me and watch over me, knowing I was about to be a new mother.... A terrified new mother.

Years passed and needless to say not a day went by that I didn't think of or miss her. The home she had lived in for years—the home we created so many memories in—had ended up in the hands of my great aunt who used it for collateral of some kind and ultimately let it end up in foreclosure—a devastating blow to the entire Fuqua family.

Seeing it boarded up and crumbling for quite some time, I finally decided, one beautiful Saturday morning, to pay it a visit one last time before it would belong to a stranger.

I called my dad and told him of my planned visit and he offered to go with me. My hope was that maybe I'd find an old flowerpot or red wagon that I could take home with me as another memory of my time with Ida Mae.

The house was locked tight, windows boarded and the secret key she kept in its hiding place was now gone, cobwebs in its place.

I wanted desperately to get inside and see, one last time, the stove she used to make her famous Mountain Dew Cakes. I wanted to see if it still smelled like "Nanny" or if maybe there was anything in there, anything at all, that I could salvage.

I do not know what made me do it, but I took my set of keys—which had my own house key, my shop key, my car key—and I began to try them, one by one, in her door.

One by one, I was defeated until... Click! My house key unlocked her door. Shocked, I took a step back in disbelief. Of all of the keys in the world and all of the locks, mine and hers matched perfectly.

I called for my father, who was equally astonished and somewhat creeped out, and we carefully entered the empty home.

Nothing felt the same. It was cold and empty, not warm and buzzing like it had been. The counter radio wasn't playing. The sun wasn't shining through some of the ugliest drapes you'd ever seen. There was no precious Ida Mae to meet me, offering me a glass of her sweet tea.

I fumbled through drawers but they were empty. The furniture was gone. Everything was gone. Except in one back bedroom, where I found a few garbage bags filled with newspapers and trash, mainly packing materials. I still ripped through them all looking to find any last trace of my great-grandmother.

In the last bag, under piles of paper, I found her old pocketbook. She carried it with her everywhere. I hugged it because it was the last piece of her I would ever have. It was light, apparently empty, but I opened it to put it to my nose in hopes it would still smell like Wrigley's gum, her favorite.

In opening the bag, I realized there were no contents, or so I thought. I caught a glimpse of something thin that I believed would be an old receipt or tissue remnant. Instead, what I found in an otherwise empty, old, thrown-in-the-trash and sitting-for-years bag, was a picture—a picture of me.

Just me.

On the same day I randomly and unexplainably decided to visit this old empty home, succeeding at using an unfamiliar key in a mismatched lock, digging through garbage only to find a treasure, there was this bag with my picture!

I believe it to be a sign. I never really believed in signs, but the feeling that came over me was more than coincidence. My great-grandmother showed me love that day, years after she had left Earth. None of that experience was coincidence. It was her leading me to something tangible that said, "I love you."

Interstitial Cystitis

Paula Bomer

9/11 was my son's first day of kindergarten at PS 38 in downtown Brooklyn. I didn't handle it well. I immediately got sick. Then sicker and sicker. It was the beginning of a slow, year-long process of evaluating every inch of my life. I lost twenty pounds. I'm five-foot-nine and I weighed one hundred and eight pounds. It was scary. I was constantly scared. I hurt so much.

I pissed blood. Freaked, I went to my midwife. It was a supposed urinary tract infection. My midwife gave me a prescription for antibiotics before the urine test came back. I took them. Later, it turned out, the test came back negative for a UTI. The pain got worse. I took over the counter drugs, which turned my piss blue. I went back on antibiotics. Peed in a cup. The test came back negative. This went on until, one time, I ran into the midwives' crowded office, crying, bent over in pain, and demanded to be dealt with. The head midwife—it was a group practice—came out and sternly told me I couldn't behave like this and I needed to see a gynecologist.

For the first time in eons, I went to a gynecologist. She was amazing. I thereafter saw her regularly. She was horrified about the endless antibiotics. She let me cry. She took my pain seriously. She said I needed to see a urologist.

The first urologist I saw in the Clock Tower near my house was a middle-aged man with Viagra flyers all over the office. He gave me antibiotics. I have a memory of visiting my parents in Austria, and sitting next to my husband, swilling down antibiotics with a large bottle of beer. I remember this because I also remember feeling ashamed and hopeless.

Weeks later, no better, I was walking down Dean Street, a block from my house, and I ran into a woman I knew from an old mothers' group that I was a part of, a group that imploded in the usual fashion of just too much bitch behavior, and she said, "Hi, how are you?"

She didn't really care how I was but I didn't care that she didn't care. I burst into a diatribe of all my bladder problems, teary and desperate. Then she said, "My husband's sister is one of the only female urologists in NYC. You should go to her." God bless that woman, an uptight middle-aged lawyer, who showed me so much kindness in that one moment. Funny how transformative even a moment of kindness can be.

I went to, who I'll refer to as, Bill's sister on the Upper East Side. She gave me a five-time supply of antibiotics. I took one course of it. The pain worsened terribly.

I went back. I was angry. I said, "It made the pain worse."

She did something which involved putting a tube in me, and there I was, in a paper gown, naked, so vulnerable, so desperate for help, and when she took the tube out it hurt, and I started to cry, and she said, "I'm sorry." And I sat down and wept.

And I said, "I always had a high tolerance for pain. When I was a little girl I broke my elbow in three places and didn't cry and no one figured it out for days until I finally turned green with pain and my mom took me to the doctor. And I gave birth twice with no drugs."

And she said, "The thing about chronic pain is it makes you more sensitive to pain. It's as if your body can't take it anymore." She was nice.

I said, "I think I have interstitial cystitis," because at that point I'd been on the Internet.

She told me to stay off the Internet. And then she said, "Go see these pelvic floor physical therapists," and gave me a prescription for it.

Did you know that the bladder is a muscle? That it can shrink or grow, like any muscle? That is can shrink to the size of a walnut? Did you know that interstitial cystitis is sort of like having ulcers in your bladder? Did you know some women who have it get their bladders removed, wear those bags to collect their urine, and *they still are in pain?*

At this point, my husband and I were barely talking. I loved him but hated how he treated me. So I also just hated him.

At one point, sitting on the porch at our house upstate, he yelled at me, getting in my face, "You're sick and you do nothing about it. It's your fault you're sick and I can't take it anymore." This, after seeing a million doctors.

I had a rare moment of calm, and I said, "You don't like it when I'm weak. And you should see a shrink. I can't always be strong for you. You're afraid."

The pelvic floor physical therapist was a bit life changing. The first time I saw her, I wept. I told her everything. Then I lied down and she put her hand inside me and massaged. Then she hooked me up to electrical stimulation. I felt a bit better. I saw her twice a week. Then, later, just once a week. I cried sometimes. She was nice to me. I loved that woman like you cannot know. I called the gynecologist and told her what was up. She was very interested. The gynecologist went out to lunch with my therapist's boss, because she was very interested in this new field of treating pelvic pain. At lunch she sat at a table next to Keanu Reeves and asked for his autograph. He was nice.

I also started seeing an acupuncturist who also did body massage. The first time I saw her, I sat across from her desk and I wept and told her everything. I've known her now for fifteen years. She gave me gentle herbs that helped. She needled me. She gave me amazing massages. I started to get better. I did a ton of yoga. I suffered and got better. Slowly, I got better. I gained weight. Slowly, not everything I ate burned my insides.

I was healed by women. Women who cared about my body. Women touching my body. Women listening to me cry, women healing me. I think I needed that, needed intense caring, needed women knowing me so intimately, touching me so intimately.

My husband saw a therapist. We went to visit his family, staying at a house nearby. His family felt that cruelty was powerful and kindness was a weakness.

I curled into a ball on the bathroom floor, crying and crying, saying "go without me." He did.

Later, I did go to his family's house. His mother whispered something hateful about my oldest son into my ear before I even got in the house. That was the last time. That was twelve years ago. And since then, our love has blossomed. I feel safe, for the most part. Safe with him now.

This morning, I was making my endless jokes about how he should leave me for a young woman because I'm forty-six and feeling it.

He said, "I love you."

I said, "No you don't," teasingly, but it's always there, the doubt. I pulled the blanket over my face because he was coming over to me, dressed for work, a little late for work because I'd blown him and then we'd fucked. He kissed my face over the blanket, maybe three times. And he said, "I always loved you. I just wasn't very good at it."

My Bristly Muse

Chris Barickman

This is way back, late 80's, after only the first time I dropped out of university and retreated to my bunker beneath my parents' house, nestled in that cozy hamlet in that New York City suburb. For something to do I'd signed up for a philosophy course at a local college while tending bar in our village tavern. As in the majority of the many service positions I've held, my boss benignly forgave my entire lack of skill in light of my general good-naturedness and, more importantly, honesty—qualities often found lacking in my co-workers.

I started the course with a profound longing for wisdom and knowledge and finished it by bullshitting my way through ten interminable pages on the philosophy of Hegel. What I now remember of Hegel is that his method of inquiry has something to do with three things. At the time I am sure I understood more, but probably not a whole lot more. Unable to focus on the paper because of the film script-in-progress upon which I was also unable to focus, I had delayed writing it until the night before it was due.

I got an A on that paper but I don't attribute this honor to my keen wit or flowery discourse, rather to the divine being who visited me during its composition.

Back in those days, my parents didn't yet have a computer at home. But my mother ran an alternative high school out of a converted church in the next village, so on this decisive night I drove to the church to write my paper on an early-model Apple computer.

As a young child I'd been terrified of the dark so I'd slept with the lights on. There was a window next to my bed and I was convinced the Wicked Witch of the West was just outside, ever leering. At bedtime each night my father had to "seal" the window shut by running his thumb around the frame.

At 46 years old I still don't like the dark and while working on this essay I was very uncomfortable with the shadows cast by and amidst the vacant school desks.

Stuck in the first paragraph, I looked up to see a pair of small, yellow eyes, six to eight inches off the ground, in one particularly gloomy shadow of a map globe atop a desk in the far corner of the nave, last in a row. Those eyes undoubtedly belonged to a creature bigger than a hedgehog, maybe a skunk or badger. I listened carefully but the creature remained motionless, the church silent but for the buzzing of my Apple IIe.

I picked up a yardstick and began to move slowly toward him, wisely hoping he wasn't a skunk. But as I reached the first desk in the row the eyes simply vanished. There was neither noise nor movement. I explored the area and walked the perimeter of the room but found no creature.

I returned to my computer and began to employ a tried and true essay-writing technique I'd acquired at high school.

Five sections:

1) say what I am going to say
2) say something
3) say something else
4) say another thing
5) say what I have said

Throughout this process, of course, I was perpetually looking and listening for my badger, for I'd convinced myself that were he a skunk, I would have smelled him. He never again appeared, but I was certain he was there. I felt his presence as I struggled through Hegel and it was impossible to concentrate on what I was writing while he was watching me.

We've all had moments, maybe mysterious days or weeks, when our beings have been permeated with an otherness more substantial than the bread we routinely eat or the circuses we often attend.

Twenty-six years and three colleges later I now see that I couldn't have, and in fact, didn't, write that paper.

Lights Out

Nicole Adams

Downtown Burlington, Vermont in the summer evenings is magical. Optimistic college kids can be heard clucking their stories of their most recent triumphs and theatrics for blocks, smoking weed rolled into clove cigarettes, eating locally-sourced free-range everything. When I was in my early 20's, that town was my oyster.

I would sit on park benches for hours, slowly sipping my coffee while watching the town characters walk by. There were the usual ones: the town crier, the psychotic homeless woman who thinks a shopping bag is her baby, the drunken man who swears he is a Vietnam vet, the soon-to-be-famous rap star, the loud teenagers with grudges that don't match their life experiences, the squealing children with their grateful parents.

The evenings were particularly magical. The rod iron vintage-inspired lights would turn on, illuminating the brick road, casting shadows of fancy chairs and decorative trees. There was nothing quite like walking up and down that street, and on this particular night, that's exactly what I did.

Amanda met me at 7:30pm. She had just finished a shift at work and I had just spent a few hours downtown getting caught up on homework reading assignments. We met at the top of Church Street and decided to walk down, visit a bar or two, and catch up on our days.

We hugged, a normal greeting, and immediately the street light casting a shadow that made our hug look like a long, skinny cannon blew out. We jumped apart, looked up, and exclaimed how strange that was.

Then, as we walked a few steps down the street, another light blew out above our heads.

Amanda exclaimed, "Holy shit! It's like you're some sort of energy vortex or something! Two lights in one night!"

We laughed at the coincidence and how I must have some sort of super power. When a third light blew out, we stared wide-eyed at each other, mouths open.

"This is really weird." I said, looking up at the dark light bulb with trepidation. "Three times can't be a coincidence, right? I mean, no other lights are out. And they only go out right as I walk under them. This is really freaky."

We walked toward the middle of the street, so as to avoid walking me under any more street lights, and relaxed our conspiracy theories as we strolled in the direction of a bar.

When the fourth light blew out, right as I was walking under it, I thought Amanda might start to cry. She sincerely looked terrified. I assured her that it must be something wrong with the electrical wiring on this street.

She started up again with her theories. "I've heard that some humans just have, like, really strong electrical currents surrounding them. Like an aura or something. I seriously think you may be one of those people. Oh my god. You really shouldn't go near a hospital. Could you imagine?! You could throw off the medical equipment."

We continued to walk, passing the bar we had intended to stop at. We discussed with earnest my newfound super power and how this could be used to better mankind.

"Maybe I could go into Wall Street and shut down some super computers!" I felt excited, I felt afraid, I felt invincible. I felt really, really special.

An hour or two must have passed as we eventually decided to just spend the time on a park bench.

"I should be heading home. Do you want me to walk you home?" Amanda asked, worried about my astounding ability to blow out street lights and how that might endanger my safety.

"No, I'm fine." I assured her. "I'll text you when I get home."

We hugged, the usual goodbye, and I stood still by the park bench for a few seconds before picking up my book bag and heading in the direction of my apartment.

I walked sheepishly under a bridal shop with its hanging light, shoulders lifted in anxiety. To my relief, and surprise, the light stayed on.

I sighed and looked up, ready to yell for my friend, to tell her that there must be some way that I can control the powers, or maybe how not every light is affected, or something about how remarkable it was that this particular light stayed on...but she was too far away for me to yell something so strange.

She was already at the Chinese food restaurant, where she walked under the bright vintage-inspired street light as it immediately blew out.

The Spins

Cathy Alter

I should preface all of this by saying: I was not high at the time. Which was unusual, given that I was high most of my freshman year of college. People said, "Are you stoned?" by way of greeting and my boyfriend Josh and I were famous for smoking bowl after bowl and then recording ourselves on his boom box as we tried to make it through Abbott & Costello's "Who's on First," Run-D.M.C.'s "Sucker M.C.'s," and once, during Passover, an entire and spectacular reading of the Haggadah complete with the four questions.

But on this particular day, I was completely without any THC in my system.

I was lying down on my bottom bunk waiting for my friends to get me for dinner. Maybe I had been studying at the library, maybe I had finished up my last class of the day, or maybe I had been sitting at my desk doing some homework. But I was most likely in a supreme state of freshman relaxation, borne out of late nights and the sheer exhaustion of being away from home for the first time, with no curfews or even the vaguest sense of how to do my own laundry.

And then, my body became an orb, tucked like a high diver's somersault. I felt my globe self leave the bed and shoot up with a gravitational pull to the ceiling light in the center of the room, where I remained, clenched into that ball, a tight ball that became more and more tight with the centrifugal force of my spinning. I could hear the high-pitched whistle of the wind in my ears like a ship's mast. I could only open my eyes at intervals, because of the sting of the wind, and when I did, I could see my dorm room in a flurry of snapshots, the bunk bed from above and then from below, my clothes hanging upside-down in the closet, the mini fridge stuck to the wall.

I had no sense of hold, my largeness or smallness, or time in general. Was I afraid? It happened too fast for me to process fear and I wouldn't have anything to which to compare the disorientation until years later when I was hit by a car while crossing the street, when sky and street merged to fuzzy images and all sound ceased except for the dull crunching in my head.

All I could hope was that this controlling force was merciful. And just as I would years later, while being hit by the car, I asked my spinning self, "When is this going to stop?"

And all of a sudden it did. With the force in which I flew, I crashed back down, skidding into the corner of my lower birth and hitting my head into a Paul Klee postcard that was taped to the concrete wall.

Right about then there was a knock on my door.

"Let's go eat," said my best friend Andrea.

I never told anyone what had happened to me that day in my dorm room. What was there to say? Our world was one of frat parties and term papers.

For the rest of that year, I continued to have strange and unsettling blips of, for lack of a better word, knowing. Sometimes I could do a parlor trick of predicting card after playing card, other times I knew just when to look across the room at my guitar as a string was snapping away from the fingerboard. But I never took flight again.

By sophomore year I had broken up with my boyfriend and stopped smoking so much pot. And although I know these weren't contributors to all the weirdness, the weirdness ended as well.

I once remember reading that kids have extrasensory perception because they haven't "turned" yet; are not conditioned to explain things away by science or humiliation. My three-year-old son Leo has started talking to an imaginary friend he calls Dee Dee (who seems quite evil—things break and people are pushed by her hand, according to Leo.) Dee Dee sleeps, he says, in the corner of his room. And I think, perhaps she does.

But occasionally I'll meet a grownup who continues the legacy of the unexplainable. Like the friend who told me about his Old Hag Syndrome. Over cocktails in a muggy basement bar, he told me that some nights he awakes to find an old lady sitting on his chest trying to strangle him. "It sounds crazy, right?" he asked. I answered, in the most normal way that I could, and started spinning my own story.

Bios

Allie Marini holds degrees from Antioch University of Los Angeles & New College of Florida, meaning she can explain deconstructionism, but cannot perform simple math. Her work has been a finalist for Best of the Net & nominated for the Pushcart Prize. She is managing editor for the *NonBinary Review*, *Unbound Octavo*, and Zoetic Press, and co-edits for Lucky Bastard Press with her man, performance poet B Deep. She has previously served on the masthead for a bunch of literary journals that you can Google & has authored 11 small-press chapbooks, including most recently *Cliffdiving* (Nomadic Press), *And When She Tasted of Knowledge* (Nomadic Press), *Southern Cryptozoology: A Field Guide To Beasts Of The Southern Wild* (Hyacinth Girl Press), *Here Comes Hell* {dancing girl press}, and *Heart Radicals*, a collaborative collection with Les Kay, Janeen Pergrin Rastall and Sandra Marchetti (ELJ Publications).

Allie rarely sleeps, and her mother has hypothesized that she is actually a robot fueled by Diet Coke and sriracha. She once met George R.R. Martin and didn't die. Does this prove immortality? Maybe not, but it does make a compelling argument. Find her on the web: facebook.com/AllieMariniBatts or @kiddeternity.

Ben Loory is the author of the collection *Stories for Nighttime and Some for the Day* (Penguin, 2011), and a picture book for children, *The Baseball Player and the Walrus* (Dial Books for Young Readers, 2015). His fables and tales have appeared in *The New Yorker*, *Tin House*, and *The Antioch Review*, and been heard on *This American Life* and *Selected Shorts*. He lives in Los Angeles, where he is an instructor for the UCLA Extension Writers' Program.

Ben Tanzer is the author of the books *Orphans*, which won the 24th Annual Midwest Book Award in Fantasy/SciFi/Horror/Paranormal and a Bronze medal in the Science Fiction category at the 2015 IPPY Awards, *Lost in Space*, which received the 2015 Devil's Kitchen Reading Award in Prose Nonfiction, and now *The New York Stories*, among others. He has also contributed to *Punk Planet*, *Clamor*, and *Men's Health*, serves as Senior Director, Acquisitions for Curbside Splendor, and can be found online at *This Blog Will Change Your Life* (bentanzer.blogspot.com), the center of his vast lifestyle empire.

Cathy Alter's articles and essays have appeared in the *Washington Post*, *Washingtonian*, *The Atlantic*, *The New York Times*, *Huffington Post*, *Smith Magazine*, and *McSweeney's*. She is the author of *Virgin Territory: Stories from the Road to Womanhood* and the memoir, *Up for Renewal: What Magazines Taught Me About Love, Sex, and Starting Over*. She lives in Washington, DC with her husband, their son, and one very fat cat. www.cathyalter.com

American singer/songwriter **Chris Barickman** has lived in Brno, Czech Republic for over a decade. He has released several folk/rock and garage rock CDs which are available all over the internet. He has published songbooks of children's and bluegrass music in Czech and is the only foreigner known to have written a song in the Czech language. In addition to his touring of bars and clubs in Europe and the States, both solo and with various bands, he busked for years on the streets of Czech and German cities as well as on Grafton Street in Dublin. He once performed for the Prince of Sweden on a navy ship docked in the Cork, Ireland Harbor. www.chrisbarickman.com

Christine Conte lives in Maine and occasionally writes stuff. She had two poems published in *Uno Kudo Volume 2*. Her current project, a supernatural comedy for lack of a better description, may someday see the light of day.

Chuck Howe is a writer, musician and humorist from Westchester, New York. His hobbies include philosophical conversations with plants and animals, and screaming at traffic. His debut novel, *Destiny Unbound* (Czuch Republic), and short story collection *If I Had Wings These Windmills Would Be Dead* (Unknown Press) are available on Amazon.

Erin Parker won her first creative writing contest when she was 11, and has been writing ever since. Her work has been published in various places by *Uno Kudo*, *Drunk Monkeys*, *Lost in Thought*, Timid Pirate Publishing, *The Altar Collective*, *Santa Fe Lit Review*, Lucid Moose Lit and Silver Birch Press. Erin was a finalist in the 2012 NGR Literary Honors contest and was nominated for Best of the Net 2014. She is an editor for *Uno Kudo* and *JMWW*. Erin is the author of a short story collection, *The Secret and the Sacred*, from Unknown Press. Visit her online at erinkparker.com.

Gay Degani has been published online and in print and won the 11th Annual Glass Woman Prize. Three of her flash pieces have been nominated for Pushcart consideration. Her suspense novel, *What Came Before*, was published in 2014, and a suspense novella, *The Old Road*, is coming out in early 2016. Founder and editor emeritus of *Flash Fiction Chronicles*, she's on staff at *Smokelong Quarterly* and blogs at *Words in Place* where a complete list of her published work can be found.

Heather Dorn is the Director of the Binghamton Poetry Project, a literary non-profit bringing free poetry workshops to the community, and will graduate from Binghamton University in Spring 2016 with her Ph.D. in English, Creative Writing. She has work published or forthcoming from the *Paterson Literary Review*, *Ragazine*, the *Kentucky Review*, *Not One of Us*, *Helen*, *Metonym*, and similar journals. More of her work can be found on her website: heatherdorn.com.

Julie Allen is an artist/illustrator currently residing in Kansas City, MO. Along with painting, she occasionally likes to tell a good story. You can read her other stories in Bud Smith's *First Time* anthology and Chuck Howe's *Too Much: Tales of Excess*. You can check out her artwork at JuliaKayDesigns.com.

Kelli Fuqua Hart is an Executive Editor at *Ocala Magazine*.

Martha Grover has been publishing her zine, *Somnambulist*, for over ten years. Her book, *One More for the People*, was published in 2011 by Perfect Day Publishing.

Martin Kleinman is a New York City story teller. He has told his tales of real New Yorkers in his short fiction collection, *Home Front*, (Sock Monkey Press 2013) and on his blog www.therealnewyorkers.com, as well as in the *Huffington Post*, and in venues all around New York City—from KGB to Union Hall.

A native New Yorker, Marty recently completed a second book on workplace innovation trends, and is putting the final touches on his second collection of short fiction, *A Shoebox Full of Money*. "The Storm" is from this new short fiction collection.

Maura O'Connell lives in Helena, Montana with her husband, two dogs, and three cats. She retired from her full-time job after 26 years, and loves not having to get up before 7 am. She and her husband enjoy traveling, hiking, camping, river kayaking, and sipping wine while admiring the gorgeous Montana sunsets.

Meg Tuite is the author of two short story collections, *Bound By Blue* (2013) Sententia Books and *Domestic Apparition* (2011) San Francisco Bay Press, three chapbooks and a poetic prose/ poetry chap w/ David Tomaloff coming out soon from Unknown Press. She won the Twin Antlers Collaborative Poetry award from Artistically Declined Press for her poetry collection, *Bare Bulbs Swinging* (2014) written with Heather Fowler and Michelle Reale. She teaches at Santa Fe Community College, is fiction editor for *Santa Fe Literary Review*, a columnist at *Connotation Press* and *JMWW*. Her blog: megtuite.com

Nate Barse is the custodian of a handsome handlebar moustache who makes sawdust to pay the bills and occasionally writes some words worth reading. His hobbies include video games, learning to play the tin whistle, and crusading against the Bureau of Bureaucracy.

Nicole Adams lives in the pastoral state of Vermont where all of the clichés are true and celebrated. She has been published in scientific journals and several literary collections and anthologies. When not working full-time as a Psychiatric Nurse Practitioner, she enjoys spending time with her friends, family, and writing.

Paula Bomer is the author of *Inside Madeleine*, *Nine Months* and *Baby & Other Stories*.

Peg Quinn's poetry has been published in numerous journals and anthologies and twice nominated for The Pushcart Prize. She paints murals and theatrical sets and teaches art in a private school in Santa Barbara, California.

Pei Yu Lin is a data analyst in Seattle. On a good day, she will have baked some bread, played tennis, eaten at a Taiwanese restaurant, and spoken to her family. On the best day, she will have done all of these things while traveling through a foreign country.

Robert P. Kaye's stories have appeared in the *Dr. T. J. Eckleburg Review*, *Beecher's*, *Pear Noir!*, *Ellipsis*, *Per Contra*, *The Los Angeles Review* and elsewhere, with details available at www.RobertPKaye.com. His chapbook "Typewriter for a Superior Alphabet" is published by Alice Blue Press. He facilitates the Works in Progress open mic at Hugo House and is the co-founder of the Seattle Fiction Federation reading series. He juggles and throws knives in the far upper left corner of the USA.

Ron Kolm is a founding member of the Unbearables. He is a contributing editor of *Sensitive Skin* and the editor of the *Evergreen Review*. Ron is the author of *The Plastic Factory*, *Divine Comedy*, *Suburban Ambush* and, with Jim Feast, the novel *Neo Phobe*. A new collection of short stories, *Duke & Jill*, has just been published by Unknown Press. He's had work in *Hobo Camp Review*, *Have A NYC 3*, the *Too Much* anthology, *The Otter* and *The Outlaw Bible of American Poetry*. Ron's papers were purchased by the New York University library, where they've been catalogued in the Fales Collection as part of the Downtown Writers Group.

Sarah Sarai became a certified auric healer in the 1970s. Rather than pursue that line of work she became an editor, teacher, writer, and lounger. Her poetry collection is *The Future Is Happy*; her poems and short stories are in *Ascent, Boston Review, Threepenny Review, decomP, Painted Bride Quarterly, South Dakota Review, Devil's Lake, The Writing Disorder*, and many other journals. She has an MFA from Sarah Lawrence, and lives in New York City in an apartment small by most standards, but capacious enough for no-longer-living relatives to stop by for a chat.

Sean Beaudoin is the author of five novels, including the zombie black comedy love story, *The Infects*, and the rude punk rock opus *Wise Young Fool*. His articles and reviews have appeared in numerous publications, including the *Onion*, the *San Francisco Chronicle*, and *Salon*. His short story collection, *Welcome Thieves*, is due March '16 from Algonquin Press.

Shawn Kilburn might write more if he didn't read so much. He lives in Portland, OR with his family. He's currently aspiring to be a professional fable writer. He also lovingly neglects the longest running and least read weblog on the internet at www.paperclypse.com.

Steven Gowin is a video producer and writer living in San Francisco.

Tantra Bensko teaches fiction writing with UCLA X Writing Program, Writers.com, Writers College, and her own Online Writing Academy. Hundreds of her pieces appear in magazines and anthologies, and several publishers have released her books. Now, she has taken charge and begun putting out her set of Psychological Suspense books (insubordinatebooks.com). They follow characters encountering bewildering events they attempt to make sense of, as we probably all have with the stories we tell here.

Wanda Morrow Clevenger is a Carlinville, Illinois, native. She has published over 334 pieces of work in 126 print and electronic publications. Her debut book *This Same Small Town in Each of Us* released in 2011. A full-length poetry manuscript is currently seeking representation.

Her magazine style blog:
wlc-wlcblog.blogspot.com/

Her About Me page:
about.me/wandamorrowclevenger

Paypal book purchase link: edgarallanpoet.com/ This_Same_Small_Town.html

Twitter: @WandaMorrowClevenger

www.ingramcontent.com/pod-product-compliance
Lightning Source LLC
Chambersburg PA
CBHW072236190626
46809CB00018B/2644